"I had no righ... ...se ... grandfat... ... I apolo...

Alexis felt as if all the ... ...ooshed out of her lungs. Not only was his apology unexpected, but the sincerity with which he delivered it was intoxicatingly endearing. She looked at Cal, his adorably tousled hair, his brilliant amber eyes, his gorgeous physique, and she knew she wasn't going to get out of this with her heart intact if he continued being nice to her.

Two weeks, she reminded herself mentally. Now that she'd reevaluated the situation, and realized it might be possible to get her mother down here and back home again before Angus even returned, all she was dealing with was two weeks.

Surely she could handle living with Cal for two weeks....

Dear Reader,

In May 2000 Silhouette Romance will commemorate its twentieth anniversary! This line has always celebrated the essence of true love in a manner that blends classic themes and the challenges of romance in today's world into a reassuring, fulfilling novel. From the enchantment of first love to the wonder of second chance, a Silhouette Romance novel demonstrates the power of genuine emotion and the breathless connection that develops between a man and a woman as they discover each other. And this month's stellar selections are quintessential Silhouette Romance stories!

If you've been following LOVING THE BOSS, you'll be amazed when mysterious Rex Barrington III is unmasked in *I Married the Boss!* by Laura Anthony. In this month's FABULOUS FATHERS offering by Donna Clayton, a woman discovers *His Ten-Year-Old Secret*. And opposites attract in *The Rancher and the Heiress,* the third of Susan Meier's TEXAS FAMILY TIES miniseries.

WRANGLERS & LACE returns with Julianna Morris's *The Marriage Stampede.* In this appealing story, a cowgirl butts heads—and hearts—with a bachelor bent on staying that way. Sally Carleen unveils the first book in her exciting duo ON THE WAY TO A WEDDING… with the tale of a twin mistaken for an M.D.'s *Bride in Waiting!* It's both a blessing and a dilemma for a single mother when she's confronted with an amnesiac *Husband Found,* this month's FAMILY MATTERS title by Martha Shields.

Enjoy the timeless power of Romance this month, and every month—you won't be disappointed!

Mary-Theresa Hussey
Mary-Theresa Hussey
Senior Editor, Silhouette Romance

Please address questions and book requests to:
Silhouette Reader Service
U.S.: 3010 Walden Ave., P.O. Box 1325, Buffalo, NY 14269
Canadian: P.O. Box 609, Fort Erie, Ont. L2A 5X3

THE RANCHER AND
THE HEIRESS

Susan Meier

𝒮𝒾𝓁𝒽𝑜𝓊𝑒𝓉𝓉𝑒
R O M A N C E™
Published by Silhouette Books
America's Publisher of Contemporary Romance

SILHOUETTE BOOKS

ISBN 0-373-19374-2

THE RANCHER AND THE HEIRESS

Copyright © 1999 by Linda Susan Meier

This edition published by arrangement with Harlequin Books S.A.

Look us up on-line at: http://www.romance.net

Printed in U.S.A.

Books by Susan Meier

Silhouette Romance

Stand-in Mom #1022
Temporarily Hers #1109
Wife in Training #1184
Merry Christmas, Daddy #1192
*In Care of the Sheriff #1283
*Guess What? We're Married! #1338
Husband From 9 to 5 #1354
*The Rancher and the Heiress #1374

*Texas Family Ties

Silhouette Desire

Take the Risk #567

SUSAN MEIER

has written category romances for Silhouette Romance
and Silhouette Desire. A full-time employee of a major
defense contractor, Susan has also been a columnist for a
small newspaper and a division manager of a charitable
organization. But her greatest joy in life has always been
her children, who constantly surprise and amaze her.
Married for twenty years to her wonderful, understanding
and gorgeous husband, Michael, Susan cherishes her
roles as mother, wife, sister and friend, believing them to
be life's real treasures. In her books she tries to convey
the beauty and importance of loving relationships.

All underlined places are fictitious.

Chapter One

Alexis MacFarland's plane left New York exactly on time. She arrived at Dallas Fort Worth Airport exactly on time. Her rental car was ready and easy to find. The directions Harvey Coulter sent to help her find her grandfather's ranch were flawless.

So, it didn't surprise her one damned bit when black smoke began billowing out of her hood, and her little white rental stopped less than five miles from the ranch. Things had been going too darned well, and, frankly, Alexis's recent luck wasn't anywhere near that good. She knew something really bad was brewing. And for a woman from New York City, being stuck in the wilds of Texas with a broken car on one of the hottest days in July, only minutes before the sun would begin to set, was about as bad as it could get. Not only was it too hot for her to try to walk five miles, but once the sun was gone she wouldn't be able to find the ranch anyway.

There was no way she was going to get out of this, she thought, popping open the car's hood and dodging the released burst of acrid smoke. She was stranded. Her luck was officially back to normal.

As if to contradict her, a open-top black Jeep appeared on the horizon. The operator drove too fast and when he pulled off the pavement, behind her white rental, his vehicle spit dust everywhere.

Alexis didn't care that he sprayed her with a dry, powdery layer of the state of Texas. She was just glad to see anyone. Relieved, she immediately began contemplating the ways she could repay him for saving her, but when he jumped out of his Jeep, all thought fled, her mouth went dry, and she instinctively understood what women felt like when they got the vapors.

Her rescuer was at least six feet tall and gorgeous. Alexis knew that if she could have found someone like him for the *Diet Splash* commercial, women all over the country would have switched brands of soda—and she wouldn't be struggling for survival right now. Because this was Texas, his Stetson wasn't out of the ordinary. Neither were the slick boots. But she hadn't expected to find a cowboy in neat black trousers and a cool, short-sleeved coral-colored sport shirt. Particularly not on a Tuesday. This wasn't what she thought a rancher would wear, and neither was it the outfit she would have chosen for him for a commercial or photo shoot, but one look in those warm amber eyes and Alexis knew clothes did *not* make the man. One smile from those full lips and her knees weakened.

His boots crunched on the pebbles and dirt of the roadside as his long-legged strides ate up the space between them. "Ma'am," he said, removing his Stetson to reveal slightly curly sandy brown hair. "Having a little car trouble?"

Dry-mouthed and rubber-kneed, Alexis pulled at her thick, shoulder-length black hair, which she knew was wilting in the heat. "It's a rental," she explained, smiling shyly, fighting to keep from falling at his feet. "And from the smoke that's coming from the engine I'd say it's over-heated.''

"I'd say you're right," the man agreed, and grinned at her, his tawny eyes sparkling. "I apologize, but I'm on my way out of town…on vacation," he confessed, smiling with self-depreciation. "I don't have a cellular phone with me, and I'm also late. So the best I can do is give you a lift to my ranch and leave you there to make your calls yourself." He offered his hand for shaking. "My name's Caleb Wright, by the way."

Alexis took the hand he extended and her lips lifted in enchantment. *So trusting.* That in and of itself was a rare treat, but it was the jolt of sexual electricity she got when his callused palm slid around her hand that made her sorry—really sorry—this was only a casual meeting.

"Thank you," she said, still smiling, still holding his hand. "I appreciate the offer of the phone. A ride over to your ranch is all I need. I don't want to keep you from your travel plans… Oh, and my name's Alexis MacFarland."

Caleb dropped her hand as if it were on fire. "Alexis *MacFarland?*"

"Yes, I'm on my way to my grandfather's ranch. He's expecting me."

Eyes narrowed, the cowboy stared at her. "He *can't* be expecting you, he's not home."

"What?"

"He's not home. He's gone fishing for two weeks. He's on his way to a cabin in the woods, and can't be reached. He didn't even take a cellular, so I know he doesn't *want* to be reached."

"But I have a letter, and papers, and a key," Alexis argued, rifling through her purse until she could produce all three.

Caleb took the documents from her hand. When the key clattered to the dry Texas dust, Alexis reacted more quickly than Cal, and bent to pick it up. Watching her long, long legs and cute derriere, he ground his teeth in frustration. He'd thought this was his lucky day. Not only had he been gifted with half of the ranch he loved, but getting to play knight in shining armor to a pretty little city slicker in a short black skirt and snug white silk blouse was definitely his idea of a lucky break. She had a body that looked like something a man would conger up in his very best dreams, and when coupled with sleek black hair, sexy green eyes and the face of an angel, Alexis MacFarland registered as close to perfect on any man's scale as a woman could register.

Unfortunately she was either a liar, or the granddaughter who'd not only deserted Angus MacFarland, but also had stayed away for eighteen long years—as punishment, as far as Caleb could tell from the bits and pieces of the story he'd heard. Either way, she was trouble.

"Angus's granddaughter left town with her mother nearly twenty years ago," Caleb said through his clenched teeth as he scanned the letter from Harvey Coulter, which looked absolutely authentic. "From the way Angus tells the story, there was an *unfixable* family split. I can't imagine anything," he said, sliding the letter behind the document, "that would make his long-lost granddaughter return home."

As he said the last, he glanced down at the paper, which was now at the top of the stack. It was an exact replica of the one Angus had given to *him* that afternoon—the agreement granting him half interest in the Triple Moors. Except where Caleb's name had been written on his, Alexis MacFarland's name was written on hers.

Angus had given *her* the other half of the ranch.

He shook her legal document at her. "What the hell is this, some kind of joke?" he asked, but he knew it wasn't. He had a paper just like this in the safe in his room.

"No, it's not a joke," Alexis gasped, but as quickly as she said the words realization dawned. Cal could see it in the expression on her face. The fear and confusion vanished from her vivid emerald eyes, and she smiled silkily. "Isn't that interesting? You say Angus is gone for two weeks?" she asked, dangling her key. "That's probably why he sent this."

"Damn," Cal muttered, and shoved his fingers through his hair. "Damn!"

"What's the matter, Mr. Wright?" Alexis asked, leaning against her disabled car. "This wouldn't by any chance mean that—as of today—you now work for a woman?"

"No," he said and narrowed his eyes at her again. "What this means is—as of today—*you and I* are partners."

Caleb Wright bounced them the entire five miles to the Triple Moors. With the top off the Jeep, wind blew above and around Alexis. Her hair knotted. Grime smudged her face. Her stomach rolled from all the jostling.

Caleb took a curve with a little more speed than was advisable, and Alexis clutched her overnight bag and peered at him. He seemed to be enjoying this.

His full, perfect lips had bowed into a wide grin, which shifted his facial muscles, accenting his high cheekbones. Sandy brown hair danced in the wind. His amber eyes shone like autumn leaves bathed in sunlight.

Yes, he was definitely enjoying this.

After what seemed like an eternity, but was probably more like ten minutes, when the sun had begun to sink and Alexis's bottom hurt in ways a true lady wouldn't mention, Caleb turned the Jeep down the long stretch of lane that was vaguely familiar to Alexis.

Part of her wanted to glance around eagerly. Another part didn't give a damn about this ranch. All it represented to her was rejection. The grandfather who was supposed to love her had kicked her mother off this ranch, then never called or wrote or visited for the next eighteen years. No, she didn't want anything to do with her grandfather, and she didn't want his ranch. But her mother wanted it—

needed it—although Rachel herself didn't yet recognize that.

The Jeep jerked to a stop in front of a house that looked about one quarter the size of the house Alexis remembered. "My, God," she gasped, not even realizing she was talking out loud. "What happened to the house?"

"Nothing *happened* to the house," Caleb retorted angrily. "Your grandfather insisted we keep it exactly the way it has always been. If it looks a little worse for the wear, it's age, nothing more."

Following his lead, Alexis gingerly exited the vehicle. There were no sidewalks. Once again dry earth greeted her five hundred dollar Italian leather pumps. A stone pierced the soft sole of her shoe and she grimaced, but, given Caleb's reaction to her comment about the house, she didn't even sigh with objection or grief.

"I'm not talking about the house's age or condition," she said cautiously, not quite sure what to make of this situation. Though ten minutes ago she'd been sorry their acquaintance would only be temporary, now that Cal had decided to cancel his trip she wasn't certain their spending time together was a good thing. Gorgeous or not, he didn't trust her. He'd come right out and told her he was staying around because he didn't want to leave her alone with the family silver— silver that she had more right to than he did—and because he had every intention of checking her out. Given that he didn't know her and she held a key to his house, she didn't think his precaution was unwarranted...but that didn't mean she was comfortable with it...

Or him.

"I was only commenting that the house seems so... *small*."

Caleb pivoted and glared at her. "*That* was whining."

"That was not whining. I merely pointed out that the house is smaller than I remember."

Walking away from her, to the back of the Jeep, Caleb

continued talking as if she hadn't spoken. "You told me you wouldn't whine. You promised that if I brought you home with me—while I tried to get to the bottom of this—you wouldn't whine. You said you didn't care how I drove, didn't care if I kept the top off the Jeep, but most of all you promised you wouldn't whine."

"I'm not whining."

He spun to face her again. Fury etched deep lines in his sun-bronzed flesh. His fair hair shone in the last rays of the sun. "I'm going to tape that voice," he said calmly, though the irate expression of his facial features didn't match his tone. "And you're going to eat those words."

For a few seconds, Alexis only stared at him. She could understand his being suspicious, but she couldn't figure out why the heck he was so angry. From what he'd told her he'd also "inherited" half of the ranch today. For an employee—probably a trusted, respected employee, but an employee nonetheless—Caleb Wright had done pretty well for himself.

Alexis drew a long breath. "Look," she said sympathetically, snagging his attention by touching his shirtsleeve as he tugged one of her bags out of the open-air compartment in the back of his Jeep. "I'm not exactly sure why you're mad, but if you're angry because you expected to get the entire ranch, not just half, I'm not going to apologize. I happen to need my stake in this ranch as much as you need yours. Your losing half its value isn't my fault…"

He threw her white leather Pullman to the powdery soil. "Is that what you think this is all about? Money?"

Seeing that her gorgeous leather bag got the brunt of his reaction to her last statement, Alexis measured her next words carefully. "Well, if you were expecting the entire ranch, you can't be too pleased to get only half. Losing half, you're losing millions of dollars."

"Lady, I don't care about millions of dollars," he said, and tossed her matching white leather tote beside the Pullman. "What worries me about this whole mess is that I think Angus is going to get hurt."

Unable to help herself, Alexis gave him a puzzled look. "*Angus* is going to get hurt? Obviously, Mr. Wright, you don't know my grandfather very well. From where I sit he does more hurting than getting hurt."

"You know what," Cal said, dropping yet another piece of her luggage to the ground. "On the drive over, I decided I didn't have much choice but to give you a chance, but you just changed my mind." He brushed his hands on the sides of his slacks. "Carry your own damned bags."

Alexis snatched up her suitcases and scrambled to catch Cal who strode toward the stairs of the wooden porch. "Look, I'm sorry," she said, confused because this ranch hand's reactions were so severe. Then she reminded herself that this wasn't any *ordinary* ranch hand. This was someone close enough, loyal enough to her grandfather that he ended up with half the Triple Moors. Like it or not, her comments about Angus offended him and, unless she wanted to sleep in the barn, explanations were in order.

"You have to see things from my perspective. I was six when my grandfather kicked us out. My entire life he had badgered my mother to get married—get a *daddy* for me," she mimicked sarcastically. "And when Mom came home and told Angus she was marrying Garret Elliott, he responded by threatening to file for custody of me. When she told him she'd fight him tooth and nail, and he'd lose, he kicked her off the ranch and told her he wanted no part of her."

They climbed the steps, but Cal still said nothing, merely led her to the front door.

"After giving Angus time to cool off," Alexis continued. "My mother invited him to the wedding, but he never came. And we never saw him again. She wrote to him for the first few years, but he didn't answer any of my mother's letters. Now, eighteen years later, he sends me a document that gives me half of his ranch, as if that's going to make everything okay. I'm sorry if it upsets you that I can't jump for joy and also that I'm more than a little bit suspicious, but I am. My guess is you would be, too. You have to admit, this whole setup looks like Angus has got something up his sleeve. I think he's trying to hurt us again…''

Cal surprised her by spinning around. He scorched her with a look that could have branded a calf—without the assistance of a hot iron. ''How the hell did you come up with that?'' he all but shouted. ''Angus spent the past eighteen years without a family, too. He suffered in silence every day. If he's doing anything here, he's trying to bring his family together, not hurt them.''

Not giving her a chance to contradict him, he added more calmly, ''Don't get too comfortable with this deal. In the first place, I read the fine print on your agreement and it says you have to live here one year before you actually take possession of your share. Frankly I don't think you'll last a year here.'' In the slight pause that followed, he glanced meaningfully at her high heels, her miniskirt and the white silk blouse, which was currently sticking to her back from the heat.

''And in the second, once Angus comes home and butts heads with you, he'll probably be sorry and take his offer back.'' With that he turned and inserted his key in the door.

Feeling properly chastised, Alexis shifted her luggage under her arms. It was easy for someone like Caleb Wright, an employee who had been more than fairly rewarded for years of hard work, to see Angus's good side. In fact, being painfully honest with herself, Alexis could even admit she knew in her heart that her grandfather probably *was* trying to bring his family back together again. But if she weren't so desperate for a way to prove to her mother that living in a loveless marriage was wrong, Angus's plan wouldn't have stood a snowball's chance in hell. Not because Alexis and her mother were unreasonable people, and not even because

Angus hadn't wanted contact with them in nearly twenty years. But because he hadn't called or visited when Alexis and her mother were nearly killed in an automobile accident on the way to Garret Elliott's home in Philadelphia. That one action clearly proved Angus didn't even care if they lived or died. They were on their own. Without so much as an option for discussion or a possible second chance, they were banished. And a ranch, or even a hundred ranches, eighteen years later couldn't make up for that pain.

"Like I said, don't get too comfortable." Cal sighed heavily, then pushed on the front door of the ranch house.

The door swung open, and Alexis's mouth dropped in dismay. The beautiful oak foyer she remembered was badly in need of cleaning. The once shiny wood had dulled with age and lack of care. The throw rugs were ragged. The nooks and crannies of the desk and bookcase were cluttered and dust covered. A glance down the hall proved the rest of the house—a fantastic two-story home lush with real wood, chandeliers, and huge windows—was in no better condition.

But, she also realized as she looked around, it was all the same. Except for an inch of dust and some wear and tear, nothing had changed.

A weird sensation enveloped her. She felt that if she would close her eyes, she could be six years old again....

"Think you can handle living here for an entire year?" Cal asked sardonically as he tossed his Stetson to a coat tree by the door, leaned against the newel post and studied her reaction.

"I've lived in worse."

Cal snorted in disbelief. "A woman like you, in a city like New York, where rich men are as thick as maple syrup on a pancake? I don't think so."

"I put *myself* through college," Alexis emphatically informed him. "My class load was so heavy I nearly starved to death my freshman year because I didn't know how to balance my schedule or my money. I know what it is to rough it. I *have* roughed it.''

"Honey, you can put your boots in the oven, but that don't make 'em biscuits.''

She stared at him. "Pardon me?''

He shook his head and turned his attention to some mail that was sitting on a table by the door. "If you didn't get that, I'm not going to explain it to you.''

Flabbergasted, Alexis took a good, hard look at Cal. Broodingly handsome, tall and broad, muscled and toned, Caleb Wright was the epitome of the kind of model she'd look for to sell *anything*—absolutely anything—to females. He had a face women would swoon over and a body that would have them sighing with desire. But he was also the most cynical, foolish—anybody who would refuse to explain a saying had to be standing on the wrong side of foolish—short-tempered man she'd ever met.

Right then and there she decided that even though he was without question the sexiest man west of the Mississippi, she didn't have to worry about spending a year with him. There was no way in hell she'd get herself mixed up with a man who was as negative as he was.

What worried her was the day Angus MacFarland returned home. If this deal meant that Alexis had to live with *him* for a year, she wasn't so sure she could do it.

But she'd handle that end of the problem when the time came. For now, she had more pressing business to attend to.

She glanced down the corridor to the left. "Is the den still back this hall?''

He didn't look up from reading the mail. "Yeah, why?''

"After I call about my rental car, I have to check in with my office.'' When he continued reading, she sniffed with disgust at his rudeness. "Thank you so much for granting me permission to use the phone.''

That got his attention. "What?" he asked, looking up. "Wait a minute. You can't call New York."

"Why not?" she asked, and grinned with pleasure at having irked him because he didn't seem to mind being rude to her. In fact, she figured now was as good of a time as any to dispense with unnecessary formalities. "For as long as I stay here, half this house is mine. I can use anything I want."

"Even if you live here the entire year and 'earn' your share like your agreement stipulates, half this house really isn't *yours*—just like it really isn't *mine*—because all the bills, like electric and telephone, come in the *ranch* name. This house is part of a business."

"Wonderful, then I shouldn't have any problem setting up shop here myself."

"What do you mean setting up shop here yourself?"

"Well, I have a business to run, too."

"Here?"

She smiled. "Here." She paused, then decided to really hit this guy over the head with the truth so there would be no more misunderstandings about what was going on. "I *will* last the full year. But, even if I don't, the agreement says that as long as I'm trying it's all half mine. The house, the den, the phone, even the phone bill in the ranch's name. Because Angus is giving me half the *ranch,* not half the house."

"I guess you're right," Cal agreed, surprisingly congenial, as he crossed his arms on his chest and leaned negligently against the door frame. "And since everything is half yours...which means it's now *only* half mine...you can't just come in here and act like a visitor. And I don't have to do all the work."

She narrowed her eyes at him. "What are you saying? Are you telling me you want me out there punching cows with you?"

"And ruin your manicure?" he asked, feigning incredulity. "I wouldn't think of it. But I would think it's only fair that you pick up some of the chores."

"Like what?" she asked, suspicious because if he really wanted to get rid of her he'd found his perfect avenue. First, she didn't have time for chores. She actually did have her own business to run. Elliott-MacFarland Advertising might be close to bankrupt, but she'd kept a few loyal clients and she planned to serve them—albeit by fax and e-mail. Second, she wasn't sure she knew how to do chores. She hadn't been on this ranch since she was six. And, at six, she didn't have to do chores.

"We haven't had any household help for a while, so I'd think taking care of the house would suffice."

She peered at the layer of dirt, the ragged carpets...the cobwebs! Good God, there were cobwebs! This house couldn't have been cleaned—at all—in the past year. She shook her head. "I haven't even seen a dust bunny since I took over my mother's business and hired a maid," she confessed cautiously. "I couldn't handle *this*."

"Then I guess you're saying you want to punch cows?"

"No, I do not want to punch cows."

"Well, it's either this or the cows," Cal said, as he carelessly plucked his Stetson from the coat tree by the door and placed it on his head. In the hat he managed to looked even more ruggedly handsome than he already was.

Luckily Alexis didn't like him.

Thinking fast about how she could possibly juggle all the household chores and still do her advertising projects, a wild, yet somehow practical, idea hit her. All she had to do was hire another maid. She smiled. "You know what, Cal, I think you're right. You continue punching cattle, I'll take care of the home front."

To her great satisfaction, she watched his eyes widen as if he didn't expect her easy acquiescence, but in the blink of an eye he was in control again.

"Okay, fine," he said, obviously thinking he was calling

her bluff and reaching for the doorknob. "I'll be back in about an hour for dinner."

She swallowed. Tonight's dinner couldn't exactly be made by a housekeeper she hadn't hired yet.

"Today's not really good for me and dinner," she said, smiling as brightly, yet professionally, as she could. "What do you say we start this bargain tomorrow?"

"What do you say you sleep in your car tonight, then?" Cal quickly countered. "If the bargain doesn't start until tomorrow, I sure as hell don't want you under my roof tonight."

"All right," she said, waving her hands to dismiss him because she saw his point. "Just go," she continued, glancing around at the room and wondering if a house that didn't get dusted could have food available to cook for supper. "I'll think of something."

"Good. Glad you see it my way," Cal said, content that though she'd taken him up on his offer, she'd fall flat on that pretty little face of hers, and lose some of that animosity before Angus returned. Actually, having witnessed her hostile attitude firsthand, Cal suspected that might have been why Angus had lured her here when everyone else was supposed to be gone. He wanted to give her time to calm down before he talked with her. Not only did that reasoning make sense, but giving someone time to cool off by making them wait was something Angus had done for as long as Cal could remember. He and Ryan used to refer to it as time in the freezer.

"I'll be back in about an hour."

With that, he opened the door, took a looping step onto the front porch and almost put his foot on a six-year-old boy.

Chapter Two

"Hey, Cal," Terry Jenkins said, craning his neck to look up at his neighbor.

"Hey, Terry," Cal said brightly, but the lids of Terry's big brown eyes rapidly blinked up and down as if pushing back tears. In the end the tears won. Before Cal had a chance to utter another sound, the little boy began bawling like a day-old calf.

"Terry," Cal said, hunkering beside the boy to try to comfort him. At eye level, he noticed the boy's straight chestnut hair was sweat streaked as if he'd run the two miles from his grandmother's home to the Triple Moors. "What's the matter?"

Tears streaming down his face, Terry sobbed noisily. "My gramma's sick."

"Sick?" Cal asked urgently. "How sick?"

"She's been sleeping all day," Terry said, then he sniffed.

"Did she wake up at all?"

Terry nodded.

"Did she say anything?"

"Yeah, she asked for water."

Because it didn't sound like Bertha was in imminent danger, Cal knew that Ryan Kelly, local sheriff and Cal's sort-of brother, was the most logical person to investigate. But with Terry sniffing and upset, Cal quickly decided the poor kid wouldn't last the twenty minutes it would take Ryan to get to the neighboring ranch from town, so Cal himself would have to do the honors. To cover his bases, he'd call Ryan on his way.

"I'll go over and see if I can't find out what's going on," Cal said, taking the child's hand and directing him off the porch and into the foyer. "For right now, though, why don't you come in?"

Terry ducked his head awkwardly as he entered the house and Cal got a shot of pity that hit him straight in the heart. Terry always had reminded Cal of himself as a child. Painfully shy, awkward, afraid of his own shadow. If there was one thing he had with this boy it was empathy.

"You see this lady here?" Cal asked kindly, pointing to Alexis. "That's Alex…Alexis," he amended, because when he glanced over at her he realized she didn't look like an Alex. Not one damned bit. This woman was every inch an Alexis. Tall, sleek, sophisticated and beautiful—even dirt smudged and wrinkled she was breathtaking. He guided Terry to walk over to her. "She'll take you into the kitchen and get you something to drink, while I go check on your grandmother."

With that Cal grabbed the cell phone from the table beside the front door and strode out into the fading light. Dialing Ryan's number from memory, he jumped into his Jeep. When Ryan's phone began to ring, Cal shoved the keys into the ignition.

"Sheriff Kelly," Ryan said.

Maneuvering his vehicle onto the dirt lane, Cal said, "Hey, Ryan, it's Cal."

"You caught me going out the door, Cal," Ryan said good-naturedly. "What can I do for you?"

"I'm on my way to Bertha Jenkins's house."

"Bertha's? Why?"

"Little Terry just showed up on my doorstep. Says his grandmother's sick."

"How sick?"

"I couldn't tell. All Terry said was that she'd been sleeping all day. She woke up once and asked for water."

"That doesn't sound like Bertha."

"No, but it also doesn't sound like she's dying, either."

"Just the same, Cal, if you're on your way over there to check things out," Ryan cautioned. "You shouldn't take Terry with you. Is there somewhere you can drop him off before you…"

"Terry's taken care of," Cal said shortly, as he bounced along the ranch lane that led to the county road.

"You left him with the hands?"

"No, I left him with…Alexis."

"Alexis? Who's Alexis?"

Not really sure he was ready to get into this, Cal cleared his throat. "Actually it's Alexis MacFarland."

"Angus's granddaughter, Alex?"

"Alexis," Cal said, correcting him. "Angus might have called her Alex twenty years ago, but I don't think she goes by Alex now. There's no way in hell this woman acts, smells, or even looks like an Alex. What she looks like is every sin I ever wanted to commit but Angus wouldn't let me."

Ryan burst out laughing. "What in the hell are you talking about?"

"Harvey Coulter came by this afternoon. Angus gave me half the ranch."

Ryan let out a low whistle. "Congratulations."

"You may not say that after you hear the rest of the story. I think he gave me part of the ranch because he didn't want me…or you or Grace to wonder about our position in his life.''

''What do you mean?''

''He gave the other half of the ranch to Alexis.''

''He gave his granddaughter half the ranch?''

''Yeah, but I got a quick peek at her documents and Angus stipulated that for her to get her share, she has to live on the ranch for a year.''

''With you and Angus?'' Ryan asked, sounding completely confused.

''Apparently,'' Cal said, driving his Jeep off the lane and onto the county road that would take him to Bertha's. ''I mean, no one asked me to move out and Angus sent her a key, so I guess Angus wants all of us to live on the ranch like one big happy family.''

''Which is why he gave you the other half of the ranch. It was his way of saying that even though he was bringing his real family back home, we were still his family, too.''

''Exactly,'' Cal agreed—and waited. From his next statement, Cal could tell Ryan had finally figured out this wasn't necessarily a good thing.

''Don't you think this is a little weird? Angus hasn't even spoken with his daughter or granddaughter in almost twenty years.…''

''And they won't speak for another two weeks, either.''

''Why not?''

''Because Angus is on his way to the cabin for fishing.''

''So, you're stuck with this woman by yourself?'' Ryan asked incredulously.

''It appears that way.''

''Did Angus set *that* up, too?''

''No. He gave me plane tickets to Anchorage. I think he wanted Alexis to have the ranch to herself for two weeks.…''

''Oh, freezer time,'' Ryan speculated knowingly.

''Time to think things through like we used to get when

we were teenagers,'' Cal agreed, then he blew his breath out on a long sigh as he turned his Jeep onto the lane for Bertha's ranch. ''Ryan, I saw her papers, I know they're authentic. They're exactly like mine. Same agreement, same format, same typeset. My guess is Angus is trying to bring his family together again. He was sending me to Anchorage to give Alexis time alone at the ranch to cool off, but I also think he doesn't want me around when he and Alexis do battle when he returns.''

''So, why don't you leave?'' Ryan asked quietly.

''I can't. I don't trust her,'' Cal said simply. He pulled up in front of the old wood-frame house, shut off his engine and removed his keys from the ignition. ''Not only do I refuse to leave a complete stranger alone in the house for two weeks, but I have a good-size gut instinct that something isn't right here,'' he continued, jumping out of the Jeep. ''Alexis is very open about the fact that she doesn't like Angus. Yet she has every intention of staying the year to get her share of the ranch.''

Ryan didn't immediately respond and when he did his words were slow, careful. ''Wouldn't you? A year from now she can sell her half for a great deal of money.''

''You think she's here for the money?''

''Why else?''

''I don't know...and that's what worries me.'' Cal paused, drew a deep breath then said, ''Ryan, I never heard the complete story of why Rachel left. I know she and Angus had a fight. I know they were always fighting. But Alexis claims her mother tried to contact Angus several times over the years, yet Angus never responded.''

''That doesn't sound like Angus. He *wants* his family back. If Rachel would have written, he would have answered. What Alexis says doesn't make any sense.''

''Maybe that's why I'm so suspicious of her.''

''How about if I run a few checks, then?''

Cal jogged up the steps to Bertha's porch. "You mean like credit rating, police record, that kind of thing?"

"For starters. Maybe something will turn up."

"That's a great idea," Cal said, embarrassed that he hadn't thought of it himself. "Thanks, Ryan. I'll owe you one."

Ryan snorted. "No. We both owe Angus one. If it wouldn't have been for the fact that he took you, me and Grace in when we were teenagers, God knows where we'd be right now. That's why we're going to stay on top of this."

"Yeah," Cal agreed. "I think we have to. Even if Alexis's story checks out, I don't think Angus is ready for the reunion she probably has in mind. There's a chip on her shoulder the size of Ohio. She's not going to kiss his cheek and thank him for bringing her home...or even for offering her half the ranch."

"Poor Angus."

"That's only the beginning," Cal said. "If she really does stay the whole year to try to get her share of the ranch, I think we're in for a hell of a wicked twelve months. But short of trying to get her to leave before Angus returns, there's not a damned thing we can do about it."

"Cal, it's not our place to get her to leave. If everything checks out, we not only have to make sure she stays, but we should also do our best to try to get along with her," Ryan gently reminded him. "This is Angus's family. His *real* family. As his adopted family, we've got to do everything we can to see that this works out for him."

"Yeah, well, that's another little problem we might be running into. As angry as Alexis is with Angus for deserting her and her mother, I'm not exactly sure how happy she's going to be when she finds out Angus replaced them."

When Cal returned from Bertha's over an hour later, he entered the house sniffing the air because he could have sworn he smelled the scents and odors of cooking. He walked through the foyer toward the kitchen and definitely smelled the charbroiled aroma of something that had burned.

Afraid of what he might find, he paused before pushing open the kitchen door, but he drew a long breath, gathered his courage and stepped inside.

The scene that greeted him caused him to stop again. Sitting at the worn maple table were Alexis and Terry. A tall glass of milk sat beside a plate containing a half-eaten cheese sandwich.

"That was good," the kid said. "Thanks."

"Well, you're welcome, Terry," Alexis brightly responded. "It isn't often that I get compliments on my cooking."

Cal could understand why. A thin haze of smoke hovered at the ceiling as if it had taken her several tries to get a sandwich that didn't burn.

Because no one had noticed he'd entered the room, Cal quietly said, "Hi."

"Hey, Cal!" Terry said, jumping off his chair and running to Cal. "How's my grandma?"

"Well, your grandmother is in the hospital."

Terry's big brown eyes filled with tears and fear. "What's wrong with her?"

"Actually she seemed okay when I left," Cal said and hunkered beside the frightened six-year-old. "But they're not sure what made her sick so they want to run some tests."

Confused, Terry looked to Alexis. She smiled. A soft, comforting smile that soothed Terry and rocked Cal back on his heels. In the time he was away he'd forgotten how attractive she was, forgotten to steel himself against the effects of her beauty.

"When someone goes into the hospital and they do tests, it's not like tests at school," Alexis gently explained. "It's more like examinations to find out why your grandma got sick.''

"Oh," Terry said, nodding his understanding.

"I'm sure she'll be fine," Cal said, rising and boosting Terry to his chair again, while he made sure to keep his distance from Alexis. "Mostly she said her stomach hurt. And that's not too bad. Usually stomachs can be fixed.''

Calm, reasonably satisfied, Terry nodded again.

"Unfortunately that also means you can't go home yet. So, if you like, you could stay with me at the Triple Moors tonight.''

Terry glanced at Alexis. She smiled and nodded, as if giving her approval, then Terry faced Cal again. "Okay, I guess.''

"Great," Cal said.

Alexis patted Terry's hand to get his attention. "Once Mr. Wright tells us which room you're using, I'll help you get ready for bed.''

"Do I have to take a bath?''

"I'm afraid so, honey.''

Honey?

The very kind way Alexis treated Terry notwithstanding, the use of the endearment brought Cal up short. Alexis MacFarland didn't look like the kind who would like kids, let alone lavish them with affection. But it appeared she more than lavished affection on Terry, and from the adoring expression in Terry's big brown eyes, she must have been spoiling him from the second Cal left to check on his grandmother. That didn't fit the mold of what he expected.

"I'll tell you what. If you allow Mr. Wright to help you with your bath, I'll read you a story.''

Terry's eyes widened. "Okay.''

She patted his hand again. "Okay.''

Still confused by Alexis's behavior, Cal helped Terry bathe, dressed him in a T-shirt his sister, Grace, had left behind, and handed him off to Alexis. Since he was already wet, Cal took a shower himself, then went to the kitchen looking for something to eat. Once again, the scene in the room stopped him cold.

Though he hadn't noticed it before, there was a plate of cheese sandwiches sitting in the center of the stove. He lifted one of the sandwiches and studied it. She must have made them for him—as had been their deal. In spite of the fact that one pan and two sandwiches had been burned beyond recognition, Cal smiled. Because of Terry's arrival, he'd expected Alexis to forget his request for dinner and give Terry a glass of cola and maybe rummage for a cookie or two, but her having made Terry a sandwich—and sandwiches for Cal, too—surprised Cal so much, he almost liked her.

Almost. He couldn't let a few burned skillets and a soft spot for kids blind him to the fact that something wasn't right here. Not only was her story different from what Cal would have guessed based on the way Angus pined for his family for the past eighteen years, but Alexis MacFarland wasn't the shy, quiet type. Cal feared that when Angus returned, she'd let him know exactly how she felt about him, his ranch and their checkered past. If Ryan hadn't reminded Cal that as Angus's adopted family the biggest part of their responsibility was to make sure she stayed so Angus would at least have a chance to try to straighten everything out, Cal probably would be thinking of ways to get rid of her right now.

After he reheated the plate of sandwiches in the microwave and poured a glass of iced tea, Cal took both to the back porch where he stretched out on the top step and leaned against the railing. When he had finished his meal, Alexis joined him.

"Would you believe Terry's already asleep?" she asked as she took a seat on the old wooden swing.

Thinking fondly of Terry, Cal shook his head. "Yeah.

His grandma's ranch is at least two miles down the road and he walked here in that blistering heat.''

"Good Lord."

Silence descended over them like the darkness that already surrounded them. With a light bump of her foot, Alexis set the swing in motion and rhythmic squeaks from the chain grinding against the hanging hook peppered the air.

"Where should I..." Alexis began at the same time that Cal said, "The way you handled..."

Both stopped. Both smiled tentatively. Cal remembered what Ryan had said about the necessity of getting along with her, and knew he was right. "You first," Cal said.

Alexis shook her head. "No, you go ahead."

"Well, I was only going to say that I was impressed with the way you handled Terry."

She stiffened. "Why? Because I don't look like the kind of woman who could care for a child?"

Trying to get along with her or not, Cal still wouldn't skirt the truth. He shrugged and casually said, "Yeah."

"I was a child myself once, you know."

"So was I, but that doesn't mean I remember how to take care of one." He paused to laugh. Shaking his head, he added, "Hell, I didn't do such a good job of taking care of *myself* when I was a kid. If it wasn't for the fact that my sister, Grace, could cook, my father and I probably would have starved."

"Yeah, well," Alexis said slowly, staring down at her foot, which continued to work the swing. "I didn't have a sister, and my mother had servants so I didn't have to cook." She glanced over at him. "But I know what it's like to be in a strange place—particularly if you feel you're intruding." She paused, watched her foot for another couple of seconds then added, "I didn't want Terry to feel like that so I went out of my way to make sure he knew he was welcome."

A minute or two passed in awkward silence, causing Cal to wonder if she didn't regret admitting as much as she had. There was a problem here, trouble. And it went beyond the quarrel with Angus. Which meant it wasn't any of his business.

"You did a fine job of making Terry feel at home," Cal said, closing the subject of her past as he settled back against the wooden porch pole again. "The only thing I can't figure out is what you read to him."

She hesitated. "I found a book."

He peered over at her. "You did? Here?" He stopped, considered, then said, "Don't tell me you read to him from one of Angus's spy novels."

"No. I found *The Cat in the Hat*."

"No kidding. Where?"

She cleared her throat. "Bottom drawer of the desk."

Cal's expression went from confused to embarrassed. Of course. The book was here because she'd lived here with Angus—before she and her mother left the ranch. Finding the book had probably been difficult... But, again, this wasn't his business.

"Sorry."

She shrugged. "That's okay. I'm surprised Angus not only kept the book, but he kept it in the same place... Of course, he probably just forgot it was there," she added accusingly.

Another strained silence reigned, as Cal tried to avoid delicate subjects and give Angus the chance to get to the bottom of things. But for Cal there were simply too many questions to ignore while he waited for Angus's return. If he was going to survive the next two weeks with his sanity, he at least had to know the basics.

Recognizing he might regret this, Cal nonetheless said, "You know, I just don't get you. If you dislike your grandfather so much why are you here?"

"The truth?"

He nodded. "I think I'd really like the truth."

Alexis sighed. From the look on her face, Cal could tell she was debating whether or not she should tell him. "This is going to sound very odd," she said hesitantly.

"Try me anyway."

Again, Alexis didn't immediately answer. Instead she studied him. Finally, as if she'd concluded the same thing he had—that if they were going to live together for the next two weeks she had to at least trust him with the basics—she said, "My mother, Angus's daughter, is in a bad marriage."

Waiting for more, Cal stared at her. When she didn't add anything further, he asked, "And that's relevant because…?"

"Because I think that if I can offer her the opportunity to come to the Triple Moors, it might shake her out of her lethargy and force her to see she needs to get a divorce."

"Your mother doesn't know she wants a divorce?" Cal asked doubtfully.

"My mother doesn't even realize she's in a bad marriage."

Even more dubious now, Cal peered at Alexis. "Maybe she's not."

"Oh, she is. She's just like that old saying about making frog soup. She's been in the pot for so long that she doesn't even feel that the water's boiling. But I'm on the sidelines, and year after year I've watched her withdraw as she's forced to accept things about her husband and her life. Now, she's withdrawn so far I know she'll never get out again unless I do something drastic."

"Like bring her back to her father?" Cal asked craftily.

Alexis laughed without any humor. "Like bring her back to the ranch. Like nudge her to remember the spirited woman she was all those years ago when she used to ride horses, fight with the ranch hands and even fly the helicopter. She doesn't do anything even remotely close to any of those now. Now, all she does is sit in her room. Sometimes she doesn't even read. Sometimes she doesn't come out for dinner.''

Like it or not, with that last explanation, Alexis's story made an odd kind of sense to Cal. He remembered his father's depressions and apathy after his mother's death, and, though he knew the two situations were entirely different, he painfully remembered the way his father withered away and died. Jackson Wright never complained. He never stopped working. He never stopped loving his children. He simply withdrew.

"How can you be so sure your mother's unhappiness is because of her marriage?" Cal asked cautiously.

"Honestly I'm not," Alexis admitted ruefully. "All I have is a hunch. But," she added more optimistically, "if you look at this logically, what I'm trying to do is pull my mother back again. Even if her withdrawal isn't the result of her marriage, it can't hurt to bring her to the place she was most alive.''

Clearing his throat, Cal shook his head. "No," he said quietly. "It can't.''

As if she'd decided she'd said enough, Alexis rose from the swing. "If you'll tell me what room to use, I'd like to go to bed.''

"You're probably going to have to use my sister Grace's room," Cal said absently. "Third door on the right.''

Halfway to the door Alexis stopped walking and faced Cal again. "Your sister Grace's room?" she asked, puzzled.

Crickets chirped, the creak of the swing died into nothing, and a few bullfrogs boasted. Cal felt as if the world came to a crashing halt.

He'd done it now. He hadn't intended to accidentally drop the bomb that Angus had created another family, but he had. And he was stuck with the consequences.

He spent at least twenty seconds pondering his options, recognizing this might be the perfect opportunity to explain a few facts like his father had died twelve years ago, Angus had adopted Grace, and both Grace and Cal had been raised like Angus's children. In the end, he concluded that this wasn't the right time because he still had the results of Ryan's investigation to weigh. But more than that, Cal considered this Angus's little drama. He might have to entertain Alexis, he might even have to make sure she stayed until Angus returned, but he wasn't going to fight the actual battle. That was Angus's responsibility.

"My sister and I lived here with Angus because our father was a hand here," Cal said, explaining without giving the whole truth. "I still refer to the room as Grace's."

"Oh," Alexis said, understanding. She smiled prettily, and Cal felt a twist in his gut. She was beautiful. Absolutely intoxicating. And *tempting*. Very, very tempting. Because he kept forgetting that, his attraction to her had a way of sneaking up on him when he least expected it.

"Well, good night, then."

"Good night," Cal said, nicely enough, but when she was gone, he rubbed both hands over his face. This was going to turn into a nightmare. He could feel it.

He didn't know how Angus was going to clear up this mess. He didn't have a clue why Angus had chosen to bring Alexis home rather than Rachel. He didn't understand why Angus bribed her with the ranch, or how the three of them would survive in the same house for an entire year.

But he did know he couldn't afford to be attracted to her.

Even if all his questions were answered satisfactorily, and the family past was settled, this woman was Angus's granddaughter. A smart man didn't sleep with the granddaughter of a man he greatly admired unless he intended to marry her.

And since Cal didn't intend to marry anyone, Alexis MacFarland was strictly off limits.

Chapter Three

Cal slept in the next morning. Because all the ranch work had been taken care of since both Angus and Cal were supposed to be out of town for the next two weeks, there was no need for Cal to get up early. He didn't have any work to do. He really was on vacation.

Elated by the knowledge that he could do absolutely anything he wanted for the first time in a long time, Cal rolled out of bed and strolled to the bathroom to take a leisurely shower. He let the warm spray pummel him into complete relaxation, thinking—as Angus had told him—that he'd better enjoy the next two weeks because when they were over, he would be half owner of a ranch. Since Cal had been an integral part of the operation of the Triple Moors for the past ten years, he had thought Angus's warning more teasing than anything else. But standing under the warm spray of the shower—naked, content, unsuspecting—it suddenly hit him why Angus has been so insistent.

Damn it!

Not only was he now fully responsible for *half* the Triple Moors, but the other half was owned by a city slicker!

He snapped off the spray with one quick motion of his hand and was out of the shower and dressed within ten minutes. He couldn't believe this. Absolutely, positively, definitely couldn't believe this.

Oh, he understood that Angus was trying to bring his family together again, and he could appreciate that—admire that, given the circumstances. But hadn't Angus realized the ramifications of giving Alexis half the ranch....

Obviously he had or he wouldn't have given Cal a vacation and warned him of misery when he returned.

Damn.

This was not going to work. Cal couldn't imagine how it could work. Granted, he'd given Alexis a few token chores to make her understand she had to pull her weight, but, Lord above, housework was such a minuscule part of the ranch that in some circles it didn't count. Then there was the decision-making process. Would he have to ask Alexis's permission before he did things? And what about Angus? Cal felt borderline comfortable running the ranch without him. In a pinch, he knew he could make do. But he'd been banking on Angus's guidance and counsel. Would he lose that now?

Like a lion hunting its enemy, Cal stormed down the steps toward the kitchen, not quite sure how he was going to handle any of this. He wanted coffee, a pastry and a well-rested horse, so he could ride for about two hours to think some of this through—Lord knew who could think confined by walls—but when he charged into the kitchen, all his problems were portrayed like a Norman Rockwell painting.

Little Terry obediently sat at the table, his hands folded primly on his lap. At the stove, Alexis wrestled with French toast. Clean and fresh from a shower, she wore jeans and a snug spaghetti-strap T-shirt. Her sleek dark hair brushed the smooth white skin of her exposed shoulders. Her jeans accented every perfect curve of her absolutely flawless backside.

Odd dizziness stopped Cal in his tracks. For a second, he thought he might have to sit. The woman was so blasted attractive he only had to look at her to get aroused. Fleetingly he contemplated conveniently forgetting she was Angus's granddaughter and letting the chips fall where they may, then he remembered prim and proper Terry, politely seated at the breakfast table. He still wore the shirt Cal had found in Grace's bureau, but in the light of morning it looked more like a nightgown than an oversize T-shirt. And the boy was quiet, subdued, like some schoolgirl.

That was it. Enough was enough. Suddenly Cal knew he could deal with the situation—unreasonable, unlikely attraction and all. Fortification, strength and pure male pride sprang up to save him.

She was making a sissy of the boy.

"What in the hell is going on here?"

Alexis turned away from the stove and smiled. Even as he got the jolt of primitive lust from just looking at her beaming face, Cal stopped it in lieu of his more important concern.

"I'm making breakfast."

Any other time, Cal might have seen some humor in the delight in her voice. But that would have probably weakened him again. Wisely he knew he had to cling to his cause.

"Are you trying to turn Terry into a girl or are you just trying to dress him like a girl?"

Alexis's face fell in complete shock. "*You* gave me that shirt for him last night."

"*Last night,*" Cal emphatically clarified. "This is morning. No boy worth his salt wants to walk around looking like a girl."

"He doesn't look like a girl!" Alexis said with a gasp.

Cal ignored her. "Terry, go upstairs and put on your shorts and T-shirt from yesterday. Then you and I will take a run over to your grandma's house and pack a few things."

Looking greatly relieved, Terry nodded eagerly. He bounced off his chair and ran from the kitchen.

"Well, I never..."

"Obviously, not. Otherwise, you wouldn't have embarrassed poor Terry by making him come downstairs looking like a girl," Cal remarked then took a seat at the table, perversely pleased that she had to serve him breakfast. It was *her* fault he was this angry and confused. Especially the confused part. That was definitely her. How was a man supposed to be partners with a woman? A city slicker. A temptress. How the hell was she supposed to fit in at a ranch, and how the hell was Cal supposed to work around her?

Yeah, Angus might have set up the situation, but Alexis was definitely responsible for the confusion.

"He did not look like a girl!"

Cal shook his head haughtily. "You have so much to learn."

He said the last as Alexis set a plate of piping hot French toast on the table in front of him. Unusually crispy around the edges, the coloring was dark enough to be classified as burned, but not so dark as to be considered inedible.

"Where did you learn to cook? In a coal mine?"

"I overcook everything. I'm afraid of germs."

He stared at her. "Germs?"

"You know. Eggs, beef, chicken, they all have those funny germs that could kill you if you don't cook everything until it's done."

"Okay, lesson one," Cal said, catching her hand when she pivoted to walk away. "Done usually means brown. Anytime anything gets black, we like to call that burned."

"I know," Alexis said, exasperated, yanking her hand away. "I just don't have my timing down yet. It'll come."

Cal smiled silkily at her. "It better because that's part of the deal."

"Now, wait a minute," Alexis argued angrily. "My

grandfather *gave* me half this ranch. Whether you like it or not I..."

"Look, kid," Cal said superiorly, happy to have the upper hand. "Your grandfather might have given you half the ranch, but that's only the beginning. Once you take over, whether that's a year from now or when Angus returns, you really do take over. And that means you have to get along with me, your partner. I say we split the work. If you don't like that, then you're not fulfilling your end of the responsibilities." He paused, contemplated, then added, "I think your learning to deal with the realities of our partnership is what Angus intended when he said you had to live here for a year."

And he did. Cal finally understood that that probably was what Angus had meant when he said Alexis had to live here a year. It was Cal's bailout. If they couldn't work together, if she couldn't handle the stress, if she *wouldn't* take her share of the responsibility, then Angus—and Cal—had a way out.

Such a wise man.

Dressed in his clothes from the day before, Terry bounced into the room. "I'm ready, Cal," he said joyfully.

"Great. Have yourself a piece of this French toast, then we'll head on over to your grandma's."

Happy, Terry nodded, crawled onto his chair and snagged himself some breakfast.

Now, things were beginning to feel the way they were supposed to feel.

"You have her doing what?" Ryan demanded of Cal. Like Cal, Ryan had wavy sandy brown hair. Because both had worked at the ranch since they were teenagers, both were well muscled and toned. Both were tall. They shared enough physical characteristics that they could have passed for brothers.

"She's cooking," Cal replied, all innocence and purity.

After taking Terry home to gather his things, then giving him a riding lesson and deliberately arriving late for lunch to put a little subtle pressure on his new partner, Cal had left Terry with Alexis and driven to the sheriff's office to let Ryan know the problem was well in hand. But instead of being reassured, Ryan had gotten uncharacteristically annoyed.

Cal couldn't understand what Ryan was so fired up about. The picture looked crystal clear to him. As far as Cal was concerned, he was only fulfilling Angus's wishes. He didn't feel he should have to defend himself to Ryan, but for the sake of peace and in the name of brotherly respect, he added, "She loves to cook."

"The woman owns a company," Ryan said incredulously, his blue eyes shooting sparks of fire. He rose from the wooden chair behind his worn metal desk and began to pace in front of the filing cabinets along the wall of the cramped sheriff's office. "A highly successful advertising company in New York City. She's used to earning tons of money. She's used to telling other people what to do. She's used to people waiting on her...and you have her fixing your breakfast?"

"That's the deal."

"You're nuts," Ryan said, aggravated. "When Angus gets home he's going to whip the tar out of you."

"What? For making his granddaughter pick up her share of the work? I don't think so," Cal said with a smirk. "As far as I can recall, Angus believes in everyone pulling their weight. I think that's why he put the one-year stipulation in her deed."

"Yeah, well, I guess we'll see who's right when Angus returns home."

"I guess we will," Cal agreed amicably. "So, what else did you find out about my new partner?"

All business now, Ryan sat again. "She's as authentic as a Susan B. Anthony dollar. Graduated in the top fifth of her class at New York University, worked her way through high school and college at her mother's side, then took over her mother's business a few months after she graduated college, and grew it from a small public relations firm to one of the biggest advertising, public relations firms in New York in less than two years.''

"Lucky her."

"Didn't you hear what I said?" Ryan asked in exasperation. "She *worked* her way through both high school and college. *High school.* In high school she was working for her mother."

"So? In high school, we were working for Angus. What else?"

Ryan sighed. "Well, something happened. I can't dig into the company's private records to see why things went sour, but they did. About January, her finances began falling apart. In June, Alexis filed for protection from creditors."

"She filed bankruptcy?"

"She filed for protection from her creditors," Ryan clarified. "Which typically means she has every intention of paying them back once she gets on her feet again."

Cal took a long breath and sat back on his chair. He liked the story about Alexis trying to save her mother, but to practical, pragmatic Cal this angle made much more sense. Alexis MacFarland didn't want the ranch, she *needed* it. "I'm sure she does have every intention of paying them back…with Angus's money."

"Jeez!" Ryan said, sounding angry now. "Why are you so down on this woman! Can't you give her a break?"

"No," Cal emphatically replied, leaning forward across the desk to make his point to Ryan. "She's my partner. Half my future depends on her. If it kills me, she'll be up to the responsibility of running that ranch by this time next year when she takes over."

"Don't you mean *if* she takes over," Ryan speculated

knowingly. "Are you sure you're not trying to run her off the range, cowboy?"

"Relax, Ryan," Cal said. "I'm on the right track here. I'm doing what I think Angus wants done."

Ryan shook his head. "I think you're meddling. You weren't supposed to be home, remember? Angus gave you a trip to Alaska."

Comfortable, composed, feeling very much in charge of the situation and what Angus wanted, Cal dismissed all Ryan's negativism with a wave of his hand. "I'm fine. Things are fine."

"You better hope so," Ryan cautioned as Cal made his way to the door of the sheriff's office. "Because if they're not, if you screw this up, you don't answer to me. You answer to Angus."

"Piece of cake," Cal said, then confidently walked out into the Texas sunshine.

He dragged his feet about returning home. Not that he was trying to make trouble for Alexis. He wasn't. He just wanted to be sure she got the real flavor for the responsibility she'd taken on. When he arrived at the ranch almost two hours later, there was a strange white van parked in front of the ranch house. Alone and bored, Terry sat on the front porch, his elbow perched on his knee, his fist holding up his chin.

"What are you doing?" Cal called to Terry as he jumped out of his Jeep.

"Nothin'," Terry replied, shielding his eyes from the sun to look up at Cal.

"Where's Alexis?"

"Workin'."

"Working on what?" Cal asked, scooping the bored child from the porch and angling him in the crook of his arm.

Terry shrugged. "House stuff. Everything's moved. Stuff is everywhere."

Cal narrowed his eyes. Stuff was *everywhere?* He always thought that when you cleaned, you made things neater, not messier. Without involving Terry in the problem any further, Cal strode across the porch and through the front door. Sure enough, stuff was everywhere.

Furniture from the living room was piled in the foyer. The desk, cabinets and chairs from the den sat right beside them. A loud, annoying hum filled the air.

"Alexis!"

She came tripping down the stairs like a young girl on her way to a birthday party. She still wore her form-fitting jeans and cool cotton shirt, but her hair was pulled into a sassy ponytail and she had headphones in her ears, which were connected to a small cassette player that hung from her waistband. Though she looked as if she was working, her appearance didn't stop the damned hum, which meant she wasn't the source of the clamor.

"Hey, hi! Come on in. Sorry about the mess," she yelled above the commotion.

"What the hell is going on?" he bellowed, half to be heard, half because yelling felt good—appropriate.

"You're getting your rugs scrubbed."

"*I'm* not getting anything."

"Sure you are. I called around and discovered the Triple Moors has a long-standing contract with a cleaning service right here in town. They even have rug scrubbing equipment. This time tomorrow this place will be so clean you won't recognize it."

"You're not supposed to hire somebody to do your work! *You're* supposed to do your work!"

She planted her fists on her hips. "Oh, really?" she asked saucily. "And who's doing your work? Right now, right at this minute, who's out on the range punching your cows? And who did it this morning? And who is going to put the cows to bed tonight?"

"You don't put cows to bed."

"Don't evade the question on a technicality," she yelled over the continuing hum. "The truth is, you haven't done a lick of work all day!"

Cal let Terry slide to the floor and the little boy wisely scrambled up the steps and to his room. Furious, pumped with angry energy, Cal strode into the living room, followed a black cord to an electrical outlet, yanked it free and stopped the almighty hum.

In the silence that followed, his ears rang. He paused to enjoy the blessed hush, but within two seconds someone yelled, "Hey! Who pulled my cord?" and Alexis Mac-Farland was on his heels.

Completely ignoring the dilemma at hand, Alexis persisted with her original question. "You're not going to put me off. I want an answer. Who is doing your work?"

"I'm on vacation," Cal spat. "Remember? This is my vacation. When I'm off vacation, then I'll do my work."

"Oh, I get it," Alexis said knowingly. "We take over the ranch on the same day, but you immediately get vacation and I have to do everything."

"You are not doing everything," Cal said as a small, irritated man stormed into the room, followed the trail of his electrical cord to Cal's hand and glared at him.

"The scrubber doesn't work without electricity."

"Yeah, well…" Cal began, but Alexis interrupted him. "Take a break, Carlos. Give me fifteen minutes of peace and quiet to explain things to Mr. Wright, then you and I will finish that filthy dining room."

In spite of the fact that she'd effectively gotten fifteen minutes of quiet in which to hash this out, something about the way she said "filthy dining room" set Cal's teeth on edge.

"You don't have to talk about my house as if it were a pigsty."

"I didn't. I only stated the truth. Besides, it's not your house anymore, it's both of ours. As far as I'm concerned, it doesn't need to be this dirty. We have a good, usable contract with a cleaning service, and they are readily available at our beck and call.''

Cal crossed his arms on his chest. "So, you don't have to do anything."

"I have plenty to do," Alexis argued, growing annoyed. "I'm about to begin the process of moving my own business down here, and I have laundry, cooking, daily cleanups," she began, counting on her fingers, "and baby-sitting Terry when the mood strikes you to abdicate your responsibility... All, I might add, while you're on vacation."

"I didn't abdicate my responsibility."

"Then what the hell would you call it, when you stride into my kitchen, dump him on a chair and announce you're going into town?" She asked, pushing wayward bangs off her forehead. "I wish you'd just get done playing lord and master around here and behave like a normal person so I could get on with the rest of my life."

Her words hit him like an arrow in his chest. *Lord and master?* All he was trying to do was make sure everything ran smoothly. "If you can't take a little discipline…"

She whirled to face him. Her skin was flushed with the emotion of the argument. Her green eyes glittered dangerously. Her full, pouty mouth had opened on an intake of air. "A little discipline?" she gasped. "You're trying to make me crazy!"

No. *She* was trying to make him crazy. And doing a damned fine job. Inches away, still angrily voicing her grievances, she stood before him all fiery, passionate woman. Strong, regal, proud. Breathtaking in appearance, incomparable in style and substance, she pulled at Cal like a restless wind pulled on a tumbleweed. Before he even realized what he was doing, he grabbed her upper arms, yanked her to him and kissed that full, pouty mouth into silence.

Chapter Four

Alexis was astonished by the power of the kiss. She'd had her share of male attention and was even engaged once, but nobody ever made her feel like this. Tingly. Alive. Energized with passion and emotion. And she wasn't talking about the anger. She realized most of Cal's irritation was the annoyance of having to fight off their attraction. She knew this firsthand because the biggest part of the problem *she* was having as she cleaned his house, made his breakfast and in general lived with him for the past twenty-four hours was staving off fantasies that she was doing all this as his wife. The man was simply so thoroughly male that he made a woman feel all soft and cuddly. She could think clearly, make rational decisions, organize, delegate and work like a professional, and still feel like a soft, sexual woman, too.

A man had to be awfully sure of himself to make a woman feel this powerful, this alive.

Caleb Wright was.

Staring into his shocked brown eyes, still clinging to his broad shoulders like a lifeline, still feeling the deep, strong thud of her heart, she wondered if it was such a good idea to be alone in the house together. He found her attractive. She found him attractive. And both were having trouble fighting it.

Even as she thought the last Terry entered the room, reminding her they had a built-in chaperon. She and Cal jumped apart as if they were two misbehaving teenagers and Carlos plugged in the rug scrubber.

Noise, confusion and blessed distraction filled the air.

Alexis swallowed. She could handle this. She *had to* handle this. Not only was Terry available to keep them in line, but she was a woman with a mission. If she wanted her mother to spend some time at the Triple Moors, to remember her youth, to remember her spunk, her drive, her determination, then Alexis had to tough this out. If she really looked at this logically, and being backed into a corner could do that for a woman, she had two weeks to get her mother down here. It wasn't the extended stay for which Alexis had hoped. But if she could convince her mother to visit while Angus was still away, maybe Alexis wouldn't have to live here the entire year. She, herself, wouldn't have to deal with Angus. And she also wouldn't have to deal with this attraction she had for Cal. He could be out of her life, too.

That stopped her. She didn't want to give him up. She hardly knew the man, but the thought of never seeing him again gave her a strange, unsettled feeling.

Which only served to prove that she had to get the hell out of here. Even if she did stay the whole year, that didn't mean she could have a relationship with Cal. Number one, he was somehow closely connected to Angus, a man she could absolutely live without. Number two, she had a business in New York City to run. Number three, there was nothing to say Cal wanted a relationship with her. He wanted to sleep with her—that was the real bottom line to the attraction—but he might not want a "relationship." And number four, they were obviously two very different people.

She was positive, upbeat, optimistic. She hadn't forgotten he was a dyed-in-the-wool pessimist, a cynic...a man who didn't want her around.

Alexis had had her full-blown, official heartbreak several years ago and knew all the signs and symptoms of setting herself up for another. She couldn't sleep with a man, live with a man, make a sort of life with a man by way of their partnership and then simply walk away because they weren't right for each other in the long-term. She wasn't made that way.

"Don't ever kiss me again," she said shakily, not even sure Cal heard her over the din of the rug scrubber.

"Don't worry. I won't," Cal said, trying to reassure her because he didn't have to reassure himself. He really, really wouldn't ever kiss her again because he knew a man could get accustomed to kissing a woman like Alexis and then he'd not only be spoiled for anybody else—normal women in the real world—but he might actually begin to compromise his principles for her.

Her body was malleable, receptive to him, almost as if she were made to fit against him. But more than that, she had soft, dewy lips that seemed to pull him deeper and deeper as the kiss went on. He could feel himself losing himself, losing touch with reality...and not caring.

And that was trouble. That was something to be nipped in the bud before it had a chance to blossom. Why? Because a man who lost himself in a woman lost himself. It seemed redundant and foolish, but it was true. A man who gave in to potent lust, who hungered after a woman, didn't have a life anymore. Sometimes he hardly had an existence. He lived day to day, at the mercy of her whim. But, worse, little by little, he shifted his beliefs until one day he woke up realizing he didn't know who he was anymore.

After all, wasn't that what he'd done with Becky Ann Quinn?

"You don't have to worry about me," he called over the scrubber. "I will never, ever kiss you again."

Cal took his dinner at the diner that night and couldn't get himself out of the house fast enough the next morning. He even stayed away at lunchtime knowing that Alexis would care for Terry.

And she did. With the house well on the way to being clean thanks to three rag-wielding employees from Maids and Braids, Alexis not only had time to phone the hospital for an update on Terry's grandmother's condition, but she had time to make arrangements for critical files to be shipped to her at the ranch, and she called her mother.

"Darling, where are you?"

Alexis tugged on a strand of her hair. This was it. The moment of truth. "Well, Mom, brace yourself. I'm at the Triple Moors."

Though it was barely audible, Alexis heard the small intake of air. "Really" was all her mother said.

"I know this is going to sound odd," Alexis said, improvising on the story she'd created to give her mother an explanation since she couldn't come right out and tell her that she'd accepted her grandfather's offer in order to bring Rachel to Texas. "But Grandfather gave me half of the ranch."

"He *what?*"

"He gave me half the ranch."

"You've seen him?"

"No, that's the funny part," Alexis honestly admitted. "Through his attorney, Grandfather offered me half the ranch on the condition that I agree to live here for a year."

"You're there for a year!"

Alexis grimaced. "If I want the ranch."

"Alexis," her mother said tiredly. "I know you need money, but humbling yourself is not the way."

"I'm not entirely sure he wants me to humble myself,"

Alexis said, defending her grandfather only because it was necessary. "He's not here. He's fishing. He won't be here for the next two weeks."

"And then what are you going to do?"

"I don't know," Alexis admitted boldly. "I almost don't care. I can be here when he returns or I can stay here for the next twelve days, enjoy the ranch, tap into some old memories, get some rest," she said, rolling her eyes as she glanced around at the housecleaning project she was supervising, thought of the files being express mailed to her and smiled at Terry who sat on a burgundy leather sofa, his elbow on the arm, his chin on his palm as he stared at her, waiting for her to complete her conversation.

But the overabundance of work wasn't the worst of her troubles here at the Triple Moors. Though Cal hadn't been around, all her senses jumped to red alert every time the door opened—almost as if she was waiting for him. Expecting him. Anticipating him like a lover. And the stupidity of it was making her nuts. The man wasn't merely stubborn, he was a chauvinist. A shortsighted, narrow-minded, temperamental oaf to whom she did not *want* to be attracted.

Which was why she had to convince her mother to come down.

"Knowing Angus is gone for the next several days, this would be the perfect opportunity for *you* to do the same. You could take some time and visit, too. I know you don't need a vacation, but aren't you curious about the ranch?"

There was a pause. A long one. Alexis squeezed her eyes shut and held her breath. Her life would be so much simpler if her mother would just accept this offer, this *opportunity,* get on a plane and visit the ranch.

"No."

Alexis deflated, but she couldn't let her mother know how disappointed she was. Her mother refused to admit to her unhappiness. If she were to discover that her daughter had gone to the extreme of accepting a bribe, living with a stranger, tending a small boy, cleaning a small disaster and reorganizing her own work schedule, Rachel would categorically deny she had a problem and insist Alexis come home. With the state of their advertising firm, Rachel would have more than a motherly right to ask her to return. She had the right as the major stockholder in Elliott-MacFarland Advertising, and Alexis's boss.

"I'm not interested," Rachel quietly stated. "That part of my life is over."

"I understand," Alexis said, temporarily acceding to her mother's decision if only because she intended to change her mind. There was no way in hell she was spending an entire year with Caleb Wright. "I'll call again soon. Or if anything comes up, you can call me. Here's the number."

She quickly gave her mother the phone number for the ranch, then disconnected the call and collapsed in the big leather chair behind the desk, the chair she remembered as being her grandfather's favorite. Burgundy leather worn soft with age enveloped her as she sank in disappointment.

"Is your mom going to visit?" Terry asked curiously.

Although she knew Cal probably wouldn't approve, Alexis had dressed Terry in crisp plaid shorts and a white shirt trimmed in matching plaid. She'd combed his poker straight hair and even spritzed it into place with her styling spray. And she insisted he wear shoes and socks...even around the house.

Alexis shook her head. "No, not yet. But we'll keep working on her," she said optimistically because she knew better than to let a setback stop her from getting what she wanted. "Let's go into town and see if we can't find something good to make for dinner."

"Okay," Terry agreed enthusiastically. "Maybe we can get some candy!"

Alexis looked down at the small boy who had been quiet, obedient and even somewhat sympathetic to her problems for the past forty-eight hours and she smiled. "I'd like that. It's been a while since I had a Gummi Bear."

Terry giggled. "I like Gummi Worms."

"Oh, yuck! Gummi Worms. Who the heck thought of that?"

"I don't know," Terry said, but he giggled again, obviously pleased that he'd nearly grossed her out. "I just know they're better than Gummi Bears."

"Hmm," Alexis said, grabbing her purse. "That's an adventure we'll save for another day."

When Cal returned home that afternoon, determined to ignore his attraction to Alexis and act like a normal human being, he discovered both Alexis and Terry were gone. He found a note on the kitchen table, which told him that they had gone to town for groceries and apologized for borrowing a car. Feeling like a heel, Cal sat at the table.

It had taken him all day, but he'd finally figured out that his treatment of Alexis was more of a frightened reaction to being attracted to her than a desire to make sure she fulfilled Angus's wishes. Ryan was right. He had her working like a slave, baby-sitting a neighbor, and cooking for him, when the truth was Angus might not want her doing anything.

So, he was going to apologize, and going to let her do whatever she wanted. For all he cared she could put on a bikini and lie in the sun if that was what she wanted to do. Well, maybe the line had to be drawn right above that, but the point was he was no longer going to tell her what she had to do, and he was going to treat her normally, politely, if it killed him.

But when Alexis and Terry returned a few minutes later, all of Cal's good intentions went flying out the window. To go to town, she'd put on white linen pants and a bright peach halter. Her hair was tied back with a peach-and-white polka-dot scarf. Little round sunglasses were perched on her nose. She looked like something off the cover of *Vogue*.

"Hi."

"Well, hello," she said, cordially, nicely. "I suppose you're here for dinner."

"Yes and no," Cal admitted ruefully. He didn't blame her for thinking the worst of him. He deserved it. But right at this minute that didn't trouble him as much as the beautiful picture the smooth skin of her back made when she turned away from him to store some groceries in the cabinet.

Angus's granddaughter, he reminded himself. *Angus's granddaughter.*

"I'm here for dinner, but not just to eat. If you're in the mood, I'd be glad to grill some steaks."

Terry whooped with delight, but Alexis turned to face him, peering at him skeptically over the black wire rim of her glasses. "I thought that was my job."

"Nothing is your job," Cal said. "At least not until Angus returns and makes his wishes known. I had no right to second-guess him the way I did. I apologize."

Alexis felt as if all the air had whooshed out of her lungs. Not only was his apology unexpected, but the sincerity with which he delivered it was intoxicatingly endearing. She looked at Cal, his adorably tousled hair, his brilliant amber eyes, his gorgeous physique and she knew she wasn't going to get out of this with her heart intact if he continued being nice to her.

Two weeks, she reminded herself mentally. Now that she'd reevaluated the situation, and realized it might be possible to get her mother down here and back home again before Angus even returned, all she was dealing with was two weeks. Surely she could handle living with Cal for two weeks.

Of course she could.

"Your apology is accepted," she said congenially. "I'll even help with dinner."

He eyed her dubiously. "What can you cook that you don't burn?"

She smiled. "Jell-O."

Mercifully Alexis changed clothes to help with dinner. When she found Cal and Terry on the patio, she wore denim shorts and a cropped white T-shirt. Her shoulders were covered, her back was hidden. All he had to deal with was her legs.

No problem…

Yeah, sure.

"So what do you want me to do?"

Ignoring her legs, Cal pretended great interest in the steak he was turning. "Is the Jell-O done?"

"It's in the fridge. I used ice cubes so it will set quickly," she answered easily. "How about if I make a salad?"

"That would work," Cal said, thinking that would keep her in the kitchen—and her legs out of his line of vision—for at least fifteen minutes, but she surprised him by bringing the rinsed salad ingredients out to the redwood patio table.

She took a chair under the bright blue floral umbrella and smiled at Terry. "Go wash your hands and you can help me tear the lettuce."

"Okay," Terry said, nodding eagerly.

When the door closed behind him, Alexis faced Cal. "I called the hospital this morning."

Cal nodded. "So did I." He peeked over at her, and found he could handle looking at her as long as he kept his eyes on her face and the conversation on a neutral topic. "What did you think?"

"I didn't know what to think. They were horribly noncommittal with me."

"Same here."

"I told Terry his grandmother was fine, but I've never liked the term 'stable.' It's okay, but it's not very optimistic."

"I know."

Because there was nothing more they could say, the sound of the steaks sizzling filled the companionable silence. Cal was happy to keep himself busy at the grill, and even marginally proud of himself because he was growing accustomed to being around her and seemingly becoming capable of behaving like a normal person. The day was warm, sunny and brilliant. Terry was taken care of. His grandmother was "stable." Angus was probably fishing comfortably, not concerned about the ranch and happy to give his granddaughter "freezer" time. And basically all was, at least temporarily, right with the world.

"I called my mother this morning."

So much for right with the world.

Slowly, uncertainly, Cal faced Alexis. "What'd she say?"

"That she doesn't want to come down. She said this part of her life is over."

Though Cal might not understand the full gamut of Angus's scheme, he did realize that Angus most likely had sacrificed his beloved ranch to get his family back together again. For that to happen, Rachel *had to* come down. The fact that Alexis had her own reasons for wanting her mother to visit the Triple Moors only made things easier.

"I was hoping I could convince her to come down this week, or maybe next, before Angus returned, but I couldn't."

Hearing the melancholy in her voice, Cal froze. In spite of the fact that Alexis's current problem was actually good news for Angus, it upset her and Cal knew what he had to do. Comfort her. Not because she needed comforting—though from the tone of her voice he was fairly certain she did—but because Cal needed to be sure she stayed. And part of getting her to stay, as Ryan had told him, was getting along with her.

Still, he hesitated. There were so many stages and interpretations of "getting along" with someone. And getting along with someone frequently opened doors that were better left closed... Oh, hell. Getting any deeper involved with her than he already was would put them in close proximity and make him want to kiss her again, or touch her, or make love...and, damn it, because she was Angus's granddaughter he couldn't do that. He could if he thought it might lead to marriage, but it wouldn't because Cal had no intention of getting married. So, out of respect for Angus, he had to keep his distance.

Of course, out of respect and appreciation for Angus, it was also his duty to comfort her. Otherwise, she might get even more distressed and leave, and then Angus's plan would be worthless. And that, Cal supposed, was the priority.

Sighing, Cal left the steaks and sat on the chair beside Alexis's at the round table. Since nothing else came to mind, he said, "Don't get yourself upset about this so quickly. Try to calm down and more or less let things happen. Sometimes when you do that," he continued self-consciously, "problems have a way of working themselves out."

Smiling appreciatively, she nodded.

Cal felt strange. On the one hand, he hated giving advice, believed he was potentially taking them to an emotional place they didn't belong, and wished with all his might that his sister Grace lived closer. On the other, he got a surge of power that Alexis had not only listened, but she appeared to have accepted what he'd said.

And that was bad. He didn't want to be involved with this woman. He didn't want to be involved with any woman—at least not long-term. Yet, it seemed as if fate kept forcing him to say and do things he knew damned well would only dig him in deeper.

And the worst part of it was, if they went too far, too fast, there would be no way out....

At least no polite, civilized way that would allow him to keep his happy home.

Chapter Five

Though Cal knew he hadn't gone overboard in comforting Alexis the day before, he still felt odd about it. Uneasy. Grace and Ryan were so good with people that Cal had never needed to get personally involved with anyone. Letting everyone handle their own problems was a nice, safe way to go through life. And he liked his life safe. Comfortable.

But Alexis MacFarland made him feel anything but comfortable. In the first place, he genuinely believed she had every intention of hurting Angus. In the second, she was too sexy for her own good, too sassy for Cal to hold his temper, and sometimes so unexpectedly vulnerable she caught him off guard.

Given that he was raised by Angus, respected Angus, *owed* Angus, being kind to Alexis—regardless of how he felt about her personally—should have been a straightforward, simple thing. But it wasn't. Because what he had really done the night before when he comforted Alexis was give her the strength to continue her efforts to bring her mother to the Triple Moors early. Which actually thwarted Angus's plan.

And that just plain wasn't right. If it killed him, Cal was going to make Ryan see that this morning.

Pushing open the door to the sheriff's office, Cal said, "Good morning, Ryan…Annabelle."

"Morning, Cal," Annabelle Parker, Cal's dispatcher/secretary, cooed gaily, as Cal entered the small, cluttered office. The room was filled to capacity with metal desks, tin filing cabinets piled high with closed files and sporadic coatracks and chairs. Sunlight filtered in through the horizontal blinds on the only window, which was behind Ryan's desk.

"How are you today?" Annabelle continued, fluffing her overdyed blond hair and fluttering her eyelashes as she smiled engagingly.

Cal returned her smile. She'd been going on like this since they were in the sixth grade, though she'd long ago married her high school sweetheart, divorced him and married a man four years her junior.

"I'm fine, Annabelle. How are you, and how's Dixon?"

"Dixon is just fine, thank you very much," Annabelle happily replied, turning her chair around as Cal took the seat in front of Ryan's desk, effectively putting herself into their conversation grouping.

Ryan and Cal exchanged a quick, covert look. In his expression, Cal communicated to Ryan that he felt what he needed to discuss shouldn't be shared with the entire community.

"Annabelle, would you mind running down to the drugstore and checking to see if Mrs. Clarkson's prescription is in yet? I promised her I'd drop it off on my way home tonight."

"I can call down…"

"Such a nice morning." Ryan interrupted. "Why don't you take a break?"

Annabelle looked from Ryan to Cal and it was obvious

she knew she'd been asked to leave, but the prospect of getting outside, among other residents of Crossroads Creek was too appealing. She grabbed her shoulder strap bag and rose. "Be back in a minute."

"Take your time," Ryan called after her as she strode to the door.

When she was gone, Cal sank into his chair. "This isn't actually confidential stuff, but I do appreciate the privacy."

"The privacy's not for you but for Angus," Ryan said, assessing Cal as he spoke. "Is there a reason *you* need some privacy?"

"No," Cal emphatically informed. "I'm trying to protect Angus, too."

"Okay," Ryan easily agreed as he leaned back in his chair. "What's up?"

"Alexis is attempting to get her mother to come down early. Like within the next week or so, while Angus is still away."

Ryan sat up. "That won't work."

"Precisely," Cal said. "But the good news is Rachel is adamant. She says she doesn't want to come down..."

"But my guess is," Ryan speculated, picking up the thought where Cal left off, "that if Alexis decides to spend the whole year here, her mother will eventually visit."

"Could be," Cal said carefully.

"So, we just have to make sure Alexis stays the whole year."

Cal fought the urge to squeeze his eyes shut with frustration. Here was another one of those contradictions. Refusing to help Alexis in her crusade to bring her mother down early actually hurt Cal more than Alexis, her mother, or even Angus. The longer it took to get Rachel to the ranch, the longer he had to be partners with Alexis. He just couldn't win.

"That's easy for you to say."

"Come on, Cal," Ryan prodded. "Why don't you just spit out whatever is bothering you?"

"You keep forgetting that if she stays, she's my partner."

"So?"

"So, I'll either have to do all the work while she gets half of everything, or she'll constantly be butting her nose into things—things she doesn't understand—wanting to make decisions she doesn't have the experience or knowledge to make and in general making my life miserable."

"Welcome to the real world."

"I have been in the real world."

Ryan snorted a laugh. "Fat chance. You've been working for a man who raised you like a son. Granted, Angus isn't the easiest man to work for and granted he made absolutely sure we had our share of discipline, but, Cal, the man loved us. He *gave* us a home, called in favors to make our lives easier, settled our fights when we couldn't...and, let's face it, he used his money and influence to help us when we didn't even know we were being helped."

"That might have been true for you and Grace because both of you were spoiled, but I..."

"Baloney. If anybody's spoiled here it's you. Grace and I went out into the real world years ago. And it's about time you joined us. Did you ever stop to think Angus hooked you up with a partner as much to educate you as to lure his family home?"

Cal scowled. Even the prospect was inconceivable. "No."

"Well, think about it. Think about how easy you've had it all these years because you never left the ranch. Then think about learning to get along with another person as your partner, because the bottom line to this is there is a very real possibility that you and Ms. MacFarland will be together for a long, long time."

The choice of words sent a shaft of something undefinable through Cal's body. There *was* a very real possibility that he could be connected to Alexis forever. Twenty-four hours a day, seven days a week for the rest of his life he would be exposed to her bedroom eyes, her endless legs, her perfect derriere...

God, he had to learn to deal with her. Not just to stay sane when he was around her, but to really deal with her. To argue with her, bargain with her, coerce her to see his way. He could not remain a drooling idiot.

"Maybe she'll leave before the year is out," Cal said, unwittingly voicing that sentiment out loud.

"You'd better hope not. Angus wants her here. You've got to keep her here, but more than that I don't think it's wise for you to get your hopes up. I did some more digging yesterday and found something interesting."

Cal sat up. "What?"

"You know how sure you were Alexis was here for Angus's money?"

Cal nodded.

"Well, you can toss that theory out. Angus left her a checking account for her use while she's here. Basically she has access to enough money to stave off her creditors for at least six months, but the only withdrawals she made were for traveling expenses and to pay for the cleaning service at the ranch."

Stupefied, Cal gasped. "Angus left her a checking account?"

"Cal," Ryan said with a laugh. "Alexis is Angus's granddaughter. She's broke. If it were one of us, Angus would be doing the same thing."

"I suppose," Cal grudgingly admitted.

"I think the fact that she didn't take that money and run is proof positive that she's here for the long haul."

"You're wrong," Cal disagreed, remembering his conversation with Alexis the day before and how it seemed that she'd more than happily leave if she could get her mother to Texas sooner. He concluded that the stashed away money was the reason she wasn't worried about losing her share of the ranch, and—to his great relief—recognized that she probably did not intend to be his partner forever.

"You realize, of course, that the checking account doesn't clear her. In some ways, I think it makes her seem all the more scheming. If she gets her mother down here within the next week, she could empty that checking account and be gone before Angus even realizes she's going."

Ryan shook his head in dismay. "You're so suspicious."

"I'm not suspicious, I'm realistic," Cal insisted, if only because Ryan couldn't seem to stay objective about her. "Besides, you can't judge. You don't even know her."

"Neither do you. You've been living with her for exactly three days. You've certainly never had an in-depth talk with her, and my guess is you've probably argued more than anything else."

Cal only grunted a noncommittal response.

"And you want to know what else I think?" Ryan asked astutely. "I think the only logical reason you keep trying to find fault with her is because you're attracted to her."

Though Cal didn't think those particular feelings had any bearing on anything, he shifted on his seat. "That's ridiculous. I'm trying to protect Angus's interests."

"Then protect them," Ryan said firmly. "Don't let Alexis get away, but above all, don't antagonize her. Like I've said all along, try to make her stay at the Triple Moors a pleasant one."

Alexis watched Cal arrive home later that day and she quickly lowered the living room curtain and ran into the kitchen so he wouldn't suspect she'd been waiting for him. She'd made a light lunch, sandwiches and fruit salad, which she planned on serving on the patio again since it was such a bright, beautiful day. But she'd also gotten herself in line. She hadn't expected him to be sympathetic to her yesterday, and it took her so much by surprise that she'd actually thought about starting to like him.

And that wasn't good.

First, if she had anything to do with it, their relationship would be short-term because she didn't want to stay at this ranch for a year   not with Angus. Second, she lived in New York. He lived in Texas. That didn't work at all. Third, she had no idea what his intentions would be if they did give in to this attraction they felt for each other. Fourth, they were opposites. Opposites might attract, but they didn't make good permanent partners.

So, sweet and understanding though he had been, she'd reminded herself that he'd only comforted her because he felt he had to, and she'd fortified herself with all the reasons they shouldn't get too friendly or too close, and she'd thought of seven or eight neutral topics they could discuss while eating, watching Terry, or wiling away the sultry Texas nights.

Now, she felt in control again.

When Cal walked into the kitchen, looking rugged and masculine in his worn jeans, chambray shirt, and Stetson, all her clever conclusions and stalwart strategies went out of her head. But she brought herself back in line by pulling out her ace in the hole. Since she knew he was attracted to her, she also realized that if he *wanted* to be attracted to her, he'd be pursuing her. Because he wasn't, she had to assume he had a very good reason for holding back. For all she knew, he might already be in a committed relationship.

Refusing to embarrass herself by being overtly attracted to a man who didn't want to be attracted to her, Alexis decided to mimic his mood—which, right now, appeared to be nonchalance. She smiled politely at him. "Terry's on the patio playing with toys we brought from his grandmother's house this morning. And lunch is prepared, if you're ready to eat."

"I had lunch with Ryan in town."

Alexis fought an unexpected stab of disappointment. If she harbored any doubts about how he felt about her, that certainly put her in her place. "Oh."

"I'm sorry," he apologized. "I guess I should have called."

Because Alexis had already decided to match his disinterest, she completely rejected that idea. Pretending indifference for him and his life, she brightened. "That's not necessary. Since I'm not much of a cook, you don't have to worry about spoiling dinner. I only made fruit salad and sandwiches. Terry and I will eat."

With that she grabbed the plate of sandwiches and took it to the patio. Cal walked out with her, bringing the fruit salad, but once he set it on the table, he strode around the high redwood fence and walked away.

For a good twenty seconds, Alexis sat staring after him. Even though that encounter started off negatively, she'd kept herself in line and it had ended well. At least she thought so. They'd had a reasonable conversation, they didn't argue, and each went his or her appropriate way.

So why did she feel so empty?

When Cal returned from work that evening, he entered the house through the basement, snuck up the back stairs and grabbed a shower and changed clothes before even attempting to see Alexis and Terry. He told himself that was because he wasn't fit company for man nor beast after working with the animals all afternoon, but he also knew that if it had been Angus and Ryan waiting for him he probably wouldn't have cared.

Walking down the front stairway, he was struck by how clean the house was. The wood floors had been polished. The chandeliers gleamed. There wasn't a speck of lint anywhere. *Grace should see this,* he thought, examining the spotless tables, sparkling lamps, and immaculate rugs. She wouldn't believe it. But as he inspected the premises, Cal also realized he didn't hear any noise, and he wondered where his two houseguests were.

"Alexis? Terry?" he called, striding through the foyer to the kitchen. "Where is everybody?"

"Out here," Alexis called from the patio.

He made his way through the kitchen, which he saw was also spotless, and he wondered if Alexis had done this or if she was making good use of the cleaning service. Either way, it almost didn't bother him. He didn't want to overburden Alexis and risk botching Angus's plan, but it was also so darned good to be in a neat, orderly home, he felt somehow rejuvenated. The house was clean. They were getting along—avoiding, ignoring and evading the sexual attraction. And another day had ticked off the freezer time. In only a week and a half Angus would be home and Cal would be free again.

Buoyed with that knowledge, he opened the sliding glass door. However, when he ventured out onto the patio his good mood immediately evaporated.

"Cal."

"Ryan," Cal said, stepping onto the stone floor. "Madison," he said, addressing Ryan's wife, a smiling blonde with laughing brown eyes, who was far enough along in her pregnancy that she wore a billowing blue maternity dress. Lacy, Madison's daughter from a previous relationship, toddled a few feet beyond the patio with Terry happily following after her, making sure she didn't fall. "What brings the two of you out here?"

"We came to meet Alexis," Madison answered easily.

"And I'm glad they did," Alexis said, motioning for Cal to have a seat under the blue umbrella of the patio table. "I made iced tea."

"Thanks," Cal said, cautiously sitting and reaching for the pitcher and a glass.

"I thought you were out on the range this afternoon?" Ryan asked shrewdly.

"I was," Cal answered.

"You don't look like it," Ryan prodded.

Cal decided to shrug this off. "I showered."

"Really," Ryan said, one notch above teasing. Cal noticed that Madison kicked her husband under the table.

"Alexis was just telling us a little about her business," Madison said to distract the brothers from fighting. "She has some impressive clients."

"I *had* some impressive clients." Alexis corrected her with a grimace. "Unless I can get the business back on its feet within the next eight months, I'm probably going to lose most of them."

"Your *Diet Splash* commercial was inspired," Madison said, contradicting Alexis. "I can't believe your clients would desert somebody with your talent because you've fallen upon hard times."

"They didn't have much choice, Madison," Alexis said. "Without capital, I had to get rid of over half my staff and I don't know how long I can keep the other half. Until I get some money, I can't have employees, and without employees I don't have any services to offer."

"I'll bet Angus would be happy to help," Ryan observed casually, but Cal held his breath. He didn't care if Ryan was testing Alexis, Cal didn't want to hear this. He didn't want to hear her berate Angus, but, perversely, he didn't want to hear that she'd happily accept his money, either.

But Alexis surprised him and only shrugged and said, "I got myself into this, I'd like to get myself out of this."

"I could float you a loan," Madison offered congenially.

Alexis shook her head. "No. I can't let you do that. I need to get myself out of this. I don't know how yet. But one way or another I have to think of something, because if I can't, I'm wondering if that doesn't prove I shouldn't be running a business this size yet. Maybe what I should be doing at this point is working for somebody else."

"Could be," Madison agreed in what Cal recognized was

her business tone of voice, but then she did a complete turnaround. "I heard you hired a cleaning service."

"I didn't have to. I investigated a little bit and found there was one already under contract to the ranch."

"That must have been Grace's doing," Madison surmised, rising from her seat. "I'd love to see what the place looks like clean."

"You're going to be astounded," Alexis said, leading Madison to the kitchen door.

But Madison stopped her. "Let me get Lacy," she said, then walked to the edge of the patio, and scooped up her daughter.

"You come with us, too, Terry," Alexis called to the little boy who perked up and scrambled across the stone floor to the sliding glass doors. "What a beautiful child," Alexis cooed at Lacy, as Madison approached her.

"I know," Madison said, balancing her toddler on her arm. Bright locks of yellow hair peeked from beneath a pale blue sun bonnet. "She's my pride and joy."

"I can understand that," Alexis agreed, unconsciously ruffling Terry's hair in a show of affection. "Can I carry her?"

"Sure," Madison said and relinquished her child.

"Isn't she adorable?" she asked Terry, who grinned and nodded eagerly. Anticipating Alexis, he rushed to the sliding door and pushed it open. She smiled. "Why thank you, sir."

Terry blushed charmingly. "You're welcome."

The second they were gone, Ryan turned to Cal. "Showered," he accused, shaking his head. "And you're trying to tell me you're not attracted to this woman."

"I never said anything of the sort," Cal emphatically denied. "If I said anything it probably would have been something more to the effect that I don't *want* to be attracted to this woman. Hell, I don't even want to *like* this woman."

"You're nuts! She's great. For someone who's never been around a child, she certainly has a way with kids."

"I don't care," Cal said, and he didn't. He couldn't pay any attention to how good and kind and sweet she was. If he did, he would be finished. "If everything works out the way Angus has it planned, she and I will become business partners. You heard how stubborn she is. Won't take Angus's money, won't take Madison's money. Wants to prove herself. Well, guess what, if her business fails and she decides to become a part of the ranch, *this*," Cal said, pointing at Triple Moors soil, "is where she'll prove herself. I'm just not quite sure I want to be involved in that."

Ryan sat back on his chair. "She does sort of seem to have a mind of her own."

"And so do I," Cal reminded Ryan. "How the hell do you think the two of us are ever going to work together?"

"I see your point."

Satisfied that he'd finally figured out the real predicament and convinced Ryan simultaneously, Cal changed the subject.

If Alexis and Angus solved their problems, or if Alexis really wanted the ranch, or if Rachel refused to come down, and Cal was forced to spend a year with Alexis as her partner, he was in big, big trouble.

He was attracted to Alexis, he didn't trust her and now he knew she was every bit as stubborn as he was. Becky Ann Quinn had been sweet and quiet and still she caused him misery and heartache. Cal couldn't even begin to fathom what a woman like Alexis could do to a man's life.

Chapter Six

Cal passed the next few days making himself scarce. He spent some time doing ranch work, but, considering that he was supposed to be on vacation, he actually spent more time with Terry. Twice he took him fishing. Most evenings they played catch. Little by little the boy was moving beyond his shyness and entertaining Cal at the same time, while Alexis kept herself locked in the den doing God knew what, trying to save her business. She didn't confide what she was working on and, in the name of self-preservation, Cal didn't ask. A calm routine had developed wherein Cal and Alexis shared baby-sitting and cooking duties, and the cleaning was handled by a woman from Maids and Braids. Cal didn't contemplate that Alexis might have been staying away from him as much as he was staying away from her. He simply considered himself lucky, until the day Terry asked to see his grandmother.

Cal looked at Alexis. Alexis looked at Cal. Both could see the guilt in the other's eyes.

"I'm sorry, Terry," Cal apologized slowly. "Really sorry. Alexis and I should have thought of this sooner."

Terry didn't say anything only hung his head. Cal felt like an absolute heel.

"I'll call the hospital today, Terry," Alexis said encouragingly as she slid one finger under Terry's chin to lift his face. "I'll find out the times for visiting hours and depending upon which of us is free, either Cal or I will take you."

"You're not coming?" Terry asked quietly.

"I'll take you if Cal can't take you."

Terry cocked his head inquisitively. "Cal's not coming?"

"No," Cal said. "I'll take you if the hospital schedule doesn't match Alexis's schedule."

Confused, Terry only glanced from one to the other. "You're not coming."

"Well, one of us will probably stay home."

"Why?"

Alexis again looked at Cal. Cal looked at Alexis. Neither seemed to know what to say.

"You want both of us to go?" Alexis asked cautiously.

Terry thought for a second, then nodded.

"All right, then," Cal said suddenly. "We'll both go." He paused and caught Alexis's gaze. "As long as that's okay with you."

Alexis managed a small smile of agreement, though she wasn't at all pleased. Not that she didn't want to go to the hospital with Terry. She did. The boy had become almost a constant companion. When he wasn't with Cal he was with her. When he wasn't with her, he was with Cal…it was no wonder Terry wanted both of them to go to the hospital with him. He counted on both of them.

But the problem was she and Cal had reached a working arrangement that kept them out of temptation's way. They saw each other at meals, the preparations for which they shared, but that was it. They didn't fight. They weren't staving off an attraction and basically had begun to like each other in that distant, pleasant one-notch-above-stranger way that sometimes worked best.

She couldn't ruin that by spending the afternoon with him.

"Thanks, Alexis," Terry said, walking over and giving Alexis a big hug, and Alexis's heart sank. How could she refuse that?

The drive to the hospital took a full hour. Though he was at first energized with the enthusiasm of finally seeing his grandmother, Terry fell asleep in the back seat of the Cadillac Cal had chosen to use to transport them.

After glancing back to check on him, Alexis whispered, "He's such a good boy."

"Yeah. He is," Cal agreed quietly.

"You know, for all the time he's been with us, he's spoken of his grandmother, he's wondered about her condition, but he's never complained."

"He's tough."

"It's more than that," Alexis said, still watching the sleeping child. "Obviously his life isn't easy. He's a little boy, living with an aging adult. From what he tells me he doesn't have much in the way of playmates...which explains why he knows how to entertain himself. But he's happy, content. No matter what I do for him, no matter what I give him, he lights up."

Alexis didn't expect Cal to answer her observations, because they were only observations but also because he was clearly trying to maintain his distance from her, so he surprised her when he said, "He does seem to thrive on attention."

Alexis smiled. "Actually he can be quite a ham. Did I tell you he put on a show for me the other day?"

Cal shook his head. "No."

"He used a blanket for a stage curtain, a broom for a guitar, put on somebody's cowboy hat and sang country songs for an hour."

Cal must have gotten a vivid image because his lips

tugged upward into a reluctant smile. "He's a real character."

"Yeah," Alexis said fondly. "He is."

"Sounds like you're getting a little attached."

"Not in a bad way," Alexis assured him. "If I end up staying around for the next year, I'd like to think I could help broaden his horizons."

"You're not going to buy him another pair of plaid shorts, are you?"

His horrified tone made Alexis laugh. "No."

"Did you think I didn't realize you'd bought him some clothes?"

"He needed a few things, I happened to be in town. I didn't go overboard."

"Never said you did."

"But?"

"But I just think you ought to be careful. If you leave, or *when* you leave, it's going to hurt him."

Alexis didn't answer Cal. In fact, she said nothing for the next several minutes because she got the distinct impression that Cal was speaking from experience. He'd tried to be casual. He'd tried to sound objective. But something had seeped into his voice. Something soft. Something vulnerable.

She looked over at the rugged man who sat only a few feet away. He was big, strong, cantankerous...and vulnerable. At first that thought didn't quite fit, but once Alexis worked it around in her mind everything became crystal clear. Cal was cynical because he'd been hurt. It made so much sense that she wondered why she hadn't seen it sooner.

Before she could comment, however, he drove the car to the door of the hospital. "Take Terry in, I'll catch up with you after I park the car."

"But you..."

He stopped her with a look. Capturing her gaze with his

sober amber eyes, he said, "I'm a big boy. I can take care of myself."

She got the picture. Loud and clear. He'd shown her a soft side, now he was reminding her he could handle himself.

Got it.

Terry's grandmother looked much older than Alexis had imagined. Tired, obviously ill, the small, gray-haired woman nonetheless brightened with joy when Terry entered the room.

"Terry!"

"Gramma!" he said, scrambling toward the bed.

"Hey, hey, be careful," Alexis cautioned. "Don't forget your grandmother is sick."

Terry obediently slowed down. When he got to the bed, he wasn't bouncing with uncontrollable energy. He was able to stop short of ramming into his grandmother.

She put her arms around him. "Boy, I missed you."

"I missed you, too," Terry said. His round brown eyes filled with tears and he began to sob. He sobbed so hard and so long, both Terry's grandmother and Alexis began to cry, too.

"Has he been good?" Bertha Jenkins asked through her tears.

Alexis nodded. "He's an angel. He doesn't give me a minute's trouble. I would have never even guessed he was so upset about missing you," she added, then dabbed at her tears, glad Cal wasn't here to see this.

"My Terry's a good boy," Bertha said, smoothing his hair.

"Yes, he certainly is," Alexis agreed, disposing her soggy tissue as Cal entered the room.

He glanced from Alexis's tearstained face, to Bertha's, to Terry's and, from his expression, Alexis could tell he almost turned around and left the room again. "What's going on here?" he asked cautiously.

"Well, Terry missed his grandmother more than he let on."

She watched Cal register a sympathetic reaction, then just as quickly as she saw it form in his eyes, he banked it. He walked over to Terry, scooped him up in his arms, took a seat on the chair beside Bertha's bed and plopped the boy on his lap. "So, how are you doing?" he asked Bertha.

She grunted. "I'm feeling poorly," she admitted matter-of-fact. "But I'm also seventy-two. Things are bound to be breaking."

"Oh, you'll be up and around in no time," Cal teased, but Alexis saw the look that passed between them. She wasn't at all surprised when Cal bounced Terry to the floor and said, "Alexis, why don't you take Terry down to the gift shop to buy his grandmother a nice present?" He drew his wallet from his pants pocket and gave Terry twenty dollars. "Anything you want," he instructed the child, who whooped for joy and ran to Alexis.

She let Terry out of the room before her, then turned to Cal. He nodded for her to go, and silently communicated that he'd find out what the real story was.

"The house she rents actually belongs to Angus," Cal said as Alexis poured them both a glass of iced tea. The trip had proved too much for Terry who fell asleep after they stopped at a roadside diner for dinner. Cal carried him to his room, Alexis dressed him in pajamas and now the adults were on the patio, hashing out the details of what was turning out to be a much more complicated problem than either anticipated. "So, she doesn't have much to do to leave town."

"Where is this daughter she wants Ryan to find?"

"New Mexico."

"Why doesn't she have an address for her own daughter?"

"She says she lost it."

Alexis didn't like the sound of that. She didn't want Terry to go back to living with a grandmother who couldn't care for him, but sending him to live with a mystery relative wasn't any better. "And where's Terry's mother?"

"Terry's mother died a few years back. That was when Bertha got custody." Cal paused, sighed. "Relax, Alexis," he soothed. "Just because this family didn't grow up with a white picket fence and a vat of money, that doesn't mean they can't care for a child."

Alexis stiffened with indignation. "I never said that."

"No, but you were thinking it."

"I wasn't thinking it. I was thinking that Terry's already lived a lonely life. He doesn't need to be uprooted and thrown into a new state."

"His grandmother is going with him."

"His *sick* grandmother is going with him."

"Where did you grow up? Sesame Street? Life isn't perfect."

"I never said that it was," Alexis replied, still indignant. "I know that better than anybody, because I went to live in a house where I wasn't wanted."

Cal snorted with disbelief. "You mean to tell me that your mother gave up her father, her life here in Texas and all her friends to live with a man who couldn't accept her child?"

"Garret wasn't thrilled that my mother was a package deal, but he accepted me. It was his parents who didn't want me around," Alexis clarified angrily.

For a few seconds Cal only studied her, thinking that this tirade of hers couldn't have been more timely since he was softening to her again. Not because she looked absolutely delectable in her short mint green shirt and little white shorts, but because she was so darned kind to Terry. Having her eloquently remind him that she had a past that didn't lend itself to selflessness also reminded him that *he* didn't have a past that lent itself to trusting and, therefore, they had to get back on the right track.

"So, you had a few unhappy family picnics," he said sarcastically.

"No. Because we lived with Garret's parents, I had eighteen unhappy years, listening to Garret's mother snipe about how naughty I was, or how sloppy I was, or how noisy I was."

"Well, Bertha's not like that," Cal assured her, trying to make just enough peace that they could live together and not so much that they'd start liking each other again. "Terry's not going to have to worry that his grandmother will complain about him...or make him feel unwanted."

"Sure, we know that about Bertha," Alexis readily agreed. "But we don't know that his aunt is going to feel the same way."

"I grew up beside this family," Cal argued, exasperated, because as far as he was concerned this was settled. "They're good people. They're normal people. They'll take good care of him."

"You didn't even know this woman's married name," Alexis reminded him, angry again. "How can you say she's good people?"

"I know the family."

Alexis sniffed with disgust. "You also know my grandfather, but you found it hard to believe...and probably still do find it hard to believe...that he deserted us."

"I don't want to get into this now."

"Of course you don't, because it proves my point."

"It proves nothing, Alexis," Cal said tiredly. "Angus is a very good man. You may not have seen that from your vantage point, but he is. And I'm sure there's a logical explanation for..."

"A logical explanation for not visiting his daughter and

granddaughter in the hospital when they were almost killed in an automobile accident?''

Cal only stared at her disbelievingly.

"That certainly doesn't fit your image, does it?'' she asked haughtily. "But that's what happened. Angus fought with my mother. We took off for Pennsylvania in the middle of the night and because my mother was sobbing, while driving through as far as she could as fast as she could, she veered into the wrong lane and we got hit by a tractor trailer.''

"Angus must not have known...''

"My mother had Garret call. He said Angus took the news quietly, but we never heard from him. Not a card, not flowers, not even a phone call to see how we were.''

All the blood drained from Cal's face. By now he'd learned to read Alexis very well and he knew she wasn't lying. "This *really* doesn't sound like Angus,'' he argued earnestly. "Alexis, I know you believe what you're telling me, but is it possible you remember wrong?''

"Remember wrong?'' Alexis asked, and laughed mirthlessly as she rose from her seat and began walking toward the sliding glass door to the kitchen. "I don't think so. You don't forget a thing like that. One day I was my grandfather's pride and joy. The next, he didn't even care that I was almost killed. Think what you like about my grandfather, but I'm speaking from a little more experience than you.''

Cal shook his head emphatically. "No, you're not,'' he insisted, confused, flabbergasted and overwhelmed all at the same time. Though it was evident by the fact that she was leaving that Alexis did not want to discuss this, Cal refused to let the conversation die. He had to defend Angus. Because if he couldn't defend Angus, then she was right. And if she was right then her hurt and pain were justified. Her *anger* was justified. She wasn't spoiled or contemptuous.

The anchor he held on to to negate every soft, vulnerable, and kind act she performed would be gone.

"Personally I think I know Angus better than anyone else in the world. Ryan may have come to the Triple Moors first. Angus may have adopted Grace. But *I've* worked side by side with him for the past fifteen years…"

Cal stopped talking because Alexis turned. A horrified expression contorted her facial features. "He *adopted* your sister."

Knowing he was too far into this to back out, Cal nodded. "Our father was a hand here. He was sick, so Angus gave him a job as a handyman around the house and let us move in. Part of the reason he wanted us here was because Ryan's parents had abandoned him, and Angus was raising him. So, Ryan and I became something like apprentice hands, while my father painted, gardened and in general tended the grounds. He died before we'd been here two years. Grace was only sixteen at the time, so though I could stay on legally because I was eighteen, Grace couldn't. The only way Angus could keep us together was to adopt her, and that's what he did."

"Let me get this straight," Alexis said shakily as she fell to a chair by the patio table. "My grandfather was out playing good Samaritan to strangers while he all but ignored his real family."

"I swear, Alexis," Cal said urgently. Emotions he hadn't counted on rose up in him before he could stop them. He could see her hurt, but he could *feel* the sense of abandonment that she'd lived with as a child and probably a teenager. He could feel the fear, the loneliness, because he'd felt them himself when he discovered his father was sick. His reasons for arguing with her quickly went from convincing her about Angus's goodness to protecting her from her own conclusions. "He wasn't ignoring you. He loved you. He pined for you…"

''He left us at a hospital to die,'' Alexis reminded Cal softly. ''I think that about says it all.''

''Are you sure Angus knew about the accident?'' Cal asked, desperate for anything when the pain in her voice twisted a knife in his gut. He didn't want to feel these things. He didn't want to like her or side with her or understand her. Because when he did he wanted to hold her. He wanted to comfort her. He wanted to kiss away the unhappy eighteen years and promise the future would be better.

''Garret swears he called.''

Cal cursed, then rose from his seat, and strode toward the barn. He felt as if he were being pursued by the hounds from hell. *Hold her. Kiss her. Comfort her.* The words had gone from whispered suggestions to shouted needs. And not hers. His. It was almost as if he *needed* to comfort her— that it would benefit *him* more than her if he would comfort her.

But he knew it wouldn't. Damn it! He'd been down this road before. He knew exactly what happened.

And he knew he couldn't handle it.

Not again.

Chapter Seven

"Right now, Ryan Kelly, the sheriff, is looking for Terry's long-lost aunt."

"That's a shame," Alexis's mother replied softly, obviously touched by the story Alexis had told her about Terry. "Such a tragedy for someone so young."

"I almost feel like opposing his being dragged away," Alexis began, but her mother interrupted her.

"Alexis, don't confuse your own feelings about leaving Texas with Terry's feelings about leaving Texas. You were going into a family you hadn't yet met. Terry is being taken to his aunt's home. There's a big, big difference."

"Not if he doesn't know the aunt."

"You don't know that he doesn't. Just because his seriously ill grandmother doesn't remember the aunt's address, doesn't mean Terry hasn't met her...or hasn't seen her in the past six months. She might have visited at Christmas. If you look at this logically, dear, it's a very lucky thing for Terry to be getting into a home with someone young enough to care for him. Because the real problem here seems to be his grandmother's age and infirmity. Not being able to remember her daughter's address is proof that Terry needs to be raised by someone else.''

Alexis sighed. ''I suppose.''

''But knowing that doesn't make you any happier,'' her mother surmised astutely.

''No, it doesn't.''

''So, how's the ranch?'' Rachel asked, plainly to change the subject.

Alexis grimaced, not quite sure she should be pleased with her mother's question. Though she was glad to have her mother interested in the ranch, she also suspected her mother had only switched topics because she didn't want Alexis getting any more upset about Terry than she already was. ''It's huge and complicated.''

''My father…your grandfather…always ran it with an iron hand, yet his men were incredibly loyal.''

From the wistful quality in her mother's voice, Alexis knew her mother was recalling the good times, not the bad. Still, in fairness, Alexis couldn't let well enough alone. One of those incredibly loyal men about which her mother spoke had inherited the other half of the Triple Moors, not merely because he was loyal, but also because Angus considered him family. If her mother was going to come down here, even if she arrived at a time when she wouldn't run into Angus, Alexis knew it was only right that she be fully apprised of the situation. Because even if Angus wasn't here, Cal was.

For about the tenth time that morning, Alexis wished with all her heart that her rental car hadn't broken down the day she arrived. Then Cal wouldn't have stopped to rescue her and he'd be in Alaska right now. Alexis's mother would be free to visit without any Angus supporters around, and Alexis herself wouldn't be furious, wondering why his leaving her the night before hurt her. She'd seen how the truth about Angus was affecting him. He was weakening. Believing her. And he didn't like it.

So what does he do? He runs—just like her grandfather had deserted her and her mother when things became too complicated.

"Mom, did you know Angus adopted a child?" Alexis asked carefully.

"What?"

"Did you know your father adopted a child?"

For a few seconds there was nothing but silence while Rachel apparently contemplated that, then she said, "No. I didn't."

"She was the daughter of a ranch hand who died. Cal, the other half owner of the ranch and Angus's adopted daughter's brother, told me that when their father died, he was eighteen so he could legally stay at the ranch, but his sister, Grace, was only sixteen. To keep the brother and sister together, Angus had to adopt her."

"That doesn't surprise me, Alexis. My father was a very compassionate man."

Hearing the casual tone of her mother's voice startled Alexis so much she spoke without thinking. "To everybody but us."

"I made my choice," Rachel reminded her daughter softly. "I chose this road. Your grandfather was very clear about what would happen if I did."

"Don't tell me you're going soft on him, too," Alexis all but groaned.

"I'm not going soft on anybody, Alexis. I've no reason to be soft or difficult anymore. I'm just tired. In fact, I'm very tired. Perhaps it's time for me to lie down."

Hearing the strain in her mother's voice, Alexis could have kicked herself. The last thing she wanted to do was cause her mother more misery or give her more reason to be distressed, but the truth was the truth. And the truth was upsetting and infuriating. Besides, Alexis didn't want to spring all this news on her mother when she visited the ranch.

Irritated, but honest, Alexis sighed. No, that wasn't really why she'd told her mother about Grace. It was part of the reason, but the real bottom line was that Alexis had gotten a surge of outrage when Cal had told her about his sister. She knew it was illogical, knew it was wrong, but she also couldn't seem to control it. She'd told her mother about Grace because she wanted her mother to agree with her so they could commiserate. Instead her mother had nearly defended Angus. Not only was Alexis all alone in her anger, but now she felt foolish and petty.

She hung up the phone disgruntled and dissatisfied and began to pace through the den. Even work held no appeal. She had to admit that knowing her grandfather had given a home to strangers was every bit as confusing as it was aggravating. On the one hand, he'd been kind enough to see that a brother and sister stayed together at a time in their lives when they needed to be together. On the other hand, he had deserted her.

His own granddaughter.

"Can I come in?"

Alexis looked over when Cal opened the door. He stood there in his typical attire of jeans and a work shirt, his hat in his hand, his sandy brown hair neatly combed. If the expression on his face was any gauge he'd come to apologize for walking away without a word, but Alexis simply wasn't in the mood. "I have work spread out all over the place. Unless you have something pressing, I almost wish you wouldn't."

"Are you sure you wish I wouldn't because of the work or because you're still mad?"

"I am not mad."

"Sure you are," Cal said, slipping into the room. "And there's a part of me that knows you probably have every right to be. I should have been more careful of how I broke the news that your grandfather had adopted my sister."

Realizing he was going to ignore the fact that he walked

away from her by focusing on her trouble with Angus, Alexis decided that at least they were on safe ground. If he apologized to her for walking away from her, he might have to admit he'd done that because he was starting to see her side, or maybe even starting to like her. Yesterday, she would have been happy to hear that. Today, recognizing how similar he was to her grandfather she didn't care to have him in her corner.

She fell to the burgundy sofa. "Don't take my side."

"All right," Cal agreed easily. "How about if I take you for ice cream?"

She eyed him suspiciously. If he wasn't here to harp at her about her relationship with her grandfather, she didn't have a clue what he wanted. "Now what are you talking about?"

"It's hot. Terry and I are going to the diner for ice cream. You're welcome to come, too, if you want."

Since she'd been here the temperature had hovered around a hundred. Air conditioning helped, but it wasn't enough. And Cal's behavior was actually neutral. He wasn't going to harangue her about her grandfather. He wasn't making lame excuses about why he ran from her as if she had the plague. And she was really sick of this den.

Alexis sat up on the sofa. "Do I need to change?"

Because he didn't often get a chance like this—at least not sanctioned—Cal took inventory. Alexis's shiny black hair fell in one flaccid, voluminous curve to her shoulders. She wore a loose-knit pink shell that wasn't tight—but it certainly was friendly—over well-structured white slacks. He couldn't really call her shoes shoes, but he could say her feet were decorated by sexy thin-strapped pink patent leather sandals.

Satisfied to have looked his fill, he grinned at her. "Hell, you're probably overdressed for the diner."

She bounced from the couch. "Great, let's go."

Cal chose to drive them in the Cadillac again—Angus's

favorite car. The car was another one of those things that was in the ranch name, not Angus's name, and Cal marveled at Angus's generosity. He had given up a great deal when he'd signed over his ranch. But Angus's benevolence wasn't news to Cal. Since the day he'd met him, Cal had never seen Angus MacFarland as anything but generous.

And that was actually the motivation for the ice cream. He couldn't stand to see Alexis so torn, so tortured. In his heart, Cal knew there was a logical explanation for why Angus never contacted his daughter and granddaughter after their accident. For the life of him Cal couldn't think of it, couldn't even imagine what would be so important, so compelling, that Angus could abandon his family, but he did know that he couldn't let Alexis stew about this until Angus returned. First, it was exactly the opposite of what Angus wanted her to do. Second, watching her grapple with her feelings was driving him nuts. The weird surge of protectiveness that had overpowered him the night before wasn't letting go. It had fired his blood and filled his dreams, and he couldn't seem to get away from it.

Having spent the day reminding himself of all the reasons he couldn't hold her, kiss her or touch her, Cal realized he was going about this all the wrong way. If he would get his mind off sex and romance, he could probably do what his instincts wanted him to do—help her fight the battles that raged within her. Instead of thinking about holding her, kissing her, touching her, he had to start thinking about talking to her, reasoning with her, pushing her to recognize the truth. That way he'd be fulfilling Angus's wishes even as he dealt with this unholy need he seemed to have to get her through this.

"So, what kind of ice cream are you going to get?" Cal asked Terry, peeking at the little boy in the rearview mirror because he was strapped in in the back seat.

"I'm thinking about chocolate."

"I'm thinking about chocolate, too," Alexis said happily,

and Cal took a self-satisfied breath. He could do this. He knew he could. He just had to keep things light, friendly.

He was lucky enough to get a parking space on Main Street, right outside the diner. Alexis didn't wait for him to open her car door, and though Cal hadn't expected her to seek that courtesy, her not waiting caused Cal to contemplate that maybe part of the battle she fought revolved around not needing anyone. Being independent. Because he'd been pushing so hard to make sure she didn't take advantage of the situation, Cal had failed to notice that she didn't really argue about pulling her weight and, instead, took it as her due. That could be because of being raised in a home where she didn't feel wanted. It might be because she was simply a spirited, independent person—as her mother had been. Or it might be because she felt odd, awkward accepting a gift from Angus. If she really did believe she'd been rejected by her grandfather, and that her step-family didn't want her, receiving gifts or favors might be completely foreign to her.

The very thought made Cal uneasy. *He'd* accepted half of her grandfather's ranch without qualm because that same grandfather had taught Cal the virtue of receiving as well as the virtue of giving. Yet, it appeared no one had done the same for Alexis. What she had been taught was to pull her own weight, to more or less pay her way, which seemed to have made her believe she wasn't special or important, but a burden.

"Don't even think you're buying," he said as he slid into the red plastic booth seat beside Terry—who was kneeling, elbows balanced on the white Formica tabletop, a wide grin on his face and a shine in his big brown eyes.

"Excuse me?"

"I said, don't think you're buying. I invited you for ice cream. This is my treat."

As he said the last, Wendy Oldham, the Longhorn's newest waitress—a recent high school graduate earning money for college in the fall—bounced up to the table. "Hi, Cal."

"Hey, Wendy," Cal said. "If I remember correctly from our discussions in the car, each of us would like a bowl of that chocolate ice cream." Then, just to cover his bases, he added, "Put everybody's on one bill and give it to me."

"You bet. One check," she said, scribbling furiously. "Nothing like a good dish of ice cream after a hot day."

"No, there isn't," Cal said, politely finishing their perfunctory conversation before she skipped off.

Though Alexis didn't argue about the bill, she'd gone back to being nervous, wary. "Do all you people know each other?"

"Yup," Cal said, nodding as he watched Wendy walk away. "Dated her oldest sister on the sly, until her parents found out." He paused, then pointed at Annabelle who sat with a gaggle of women in a booth at the opposite end of the big, one-room diner. "That woman's had a crush on me since we were in the sixth grade. The two women on the other side of her booth own the newspaper. And the guy at the counter who keeps glancing over has been having an affair for the past eight years with the blonde seated beside Annabelle."

Alexis narrowed her eyes at him. "How do you know?"

Cal leaned forward across the table and whispered, "Body language."

"Yeah, well, smarty pants, if that's true, why don't they just get married?"

"They're already married—and not to each other. Hence, the affair," Cal explained teasingly, but in a voice too quiet for Terry to hear.

Alexis also lowered her voice. "That's ridiculous. If what you said was true, they'd just get a divorce and marry each other."

"Maybe in New York, but not in Crossroads Creek."

"Do you mean to tell me your people would rather commit adultery than divorce?"

"Never said we were right," Cal admitted through a chuckle. "Also never said we were proud of everything we do."

Alexis couldn't help it, she laughed at him. "You're insane."

"You bet," Cal said, settling back in the booth, comfortable that Alexis was not only relaxed enough that she might be receptive to his interference but also that he could let Terry in on the conversation. "And very happy to be here. I don't plan on taking my life too seriously, Alexis. Maybe you should lighten up about yours."

"You don't know anything about my life."

Wendy arrived with their ice cream. She set the three bowls on the table, distributed utensils and napkins, then discreetly slid the bill to Cal.

Since Alexis seemed too preoccupied to notice the bill, Cal stashed it in his shirt pocket. "Actually you've told me quite a lot. You're mad at your grandfather. You love your mother. Your stepfamily thought you were noisy. You put yourself through college. And you're too stubborn to take anybody's help to bail out your company. You're strong, independent, smart and bullheaded, but you have an incredibly soft heart."

Alexis stopped her spoon midway to her lips. "What are you, psychic?"

Cal shook his head. "Nope, just a listener."

"Obviously a good listener," Alexis admitted quietly. "I'm twenty-four years old and I've been called a lot of things like stubborn, willful, crafty and even strong, but no one gets the part about the soft heart."

"Actually, Alexis, you weren't all that hard to read. You're very much like your grandfather."

"I know you mean that as a compliment, Cal," Alexis said, but this time when her spoon stopped, she set it on the table and Cal knew she wouldn't be picking it up again. "But I don't want to talk about this with you."

"Why? Why are you afraid to hear what I have to say?"

At that Alexis drew a long, patient breath. Part of her wanted to explain to Cal that she probably would have been very glad for his help last night, but tonight, given that he'd walked out on her, he was the last person from whom she wanted advice. As far as she was concerned, he was no better than her grandfather.

"I'm not afraid of anything. I'm not even afraid of facing Angus when and if the time comes. Because all he has to do is explain why he'd leave me and my mother alone when he was told we might be dying. If he can explain that," she said, rising from her seat. "Then I'll be all ears to hear anything he has to say." She shoved her hand into her pants pocket and pulled out a five dollar bill. "If you don't need all this for my share of the check, leave the balance for a tip. I'm going outside for a breath of fresh air."

He heard her prowling downstairs in the middle of the night. Common sense told him to stay exactly where he was. His other sense, that sense that genuinely felt he was on crusade, sent him reaching for a pair of jeans and then urged him out of his room.

He found her in the den. "What are you doing up?"

Over her anger, and apparently recognizing that because they lived together they couldn't ignore each other, she sighed heavily. "Thinking."

"About what?"

"My company is on the verge of bankruptcy, and I'm this close," she said, showing him a fraction of an inch of space between her thumb and forefinger, "to an idea for the new *Diet Splash* campaign, but for some damned reason or another I'm blocked."

He stepped into the room. "If you're blocked, how do you know you're close to an idea?"

"It's an instinct," she said, then shook her head furiously as she paced in front of the old, worn desk. He got the impression that if she could have found a cigarette, she would have lighted it. "No. It's more than an instinct. When you're about to get a good idea," she explained logically, "you can almost feel it sitting on the edge of your brain. With a little time and a little prodding you shake it loose."

He grimaced. "Sounds painful."

"Oh, no, it's wonderful," she said, her eyes gleaming such a bright green they could have lit the room. "But right now I can't shake it loose."

Cal took a seat on the leather sofa, resting his arm along its back, watching the magnificent picture she made. Her hair fell loose and free. Her feet were bare. She wore an old, worn pair of jeans and a tight T-shirt.

She also wasn't wearing a bra.

But he could tell this was Alexis at her best. Restless. Driven. She virtually oozed the creativity she talked about, but he could see also she wasn't in touch with it. She *was* blocked. Cal had a very good idea of why, but after their discussions this evening he knew it wasn't his place to tell her, and he also sensed that this wasn't a process in which one intruded. Even sitting in the room with her, he almost felt as if he were stepping on sacred artistic ground.

All over a half-naked man and a diet soda.

Amazing.

"You're trying to sell soda to thirsty women, right?"

She sighed heavily. "It's not that pedestrian," she said, leaning around him from the back of the sofa and looking right in his face. He'd never thought a woman working could be so attractive, but this woman was. She was alive, powerful, sexy. Cal felt the electricity of her energy the whole way to his toes. She was trying to intimidate him, he knew that. But he refused to back down. A force equally as strong as the one she projected surged through him.

"It's much, much more involved. The women who watch

and read these ads find this man attractive. He keeps himself in shape. That's why he's drinking diet soda. They want to be someone he'd be attracted to, so they, too, drink diet soda." She spun away and began to pace again. "But there's a subliminal message for men, too. If you want to be someone women swoon over, drink diet soda."

Though he tried to stop the bubble of laughter, he couldn't. "Boy, you really sell people a bill of goods, don't you?"

Angry, she faced him. "No. We don't sell anybody anything they don't already know. We simply put it in the form that's the most quickly, most easily understood."

Looking at the fantastic picture she made, blatant sexuality coupled with restless power begging for an outlet, Cal recognized exactly what she was saying. He could almost taste how delicious she'd be in bed. "So, you use sex to sell?"

"Sometimes."

"Why?"

"Because it's the one thing everybody's interested in. Men *and* women."

He rose, followed her as she agitatedly prowled to the other end of the room, and was right behind her when she turned. "Would you use sex to sell me a diet soda?"

Barefoot and shirtless, wearing only a pair of unsnapped jeans, he stood in front of her. Alexis felt a fission of heat skitter along her nerve endings. She wouldn't use sex to sell anything to this man because it wouldn't work. First, he had enough sex appeal to keep him for the next fifty or sixty years. Second, she sincerely doubted he worried about finding ways to get women interested in him. Third, if he wanted a woman interested in him, he'd pick the woman.

Oddly enough, she felt as if he'd just picked her.

She swallowed. "No."

He stepped closer. "Why not?"

"Well, because you're very..." She drew a shallow

breath. *Sexy.* She almost said it, but knew better than to walk into that kind of trap. "Sure of yourself."

"You think so?" he asked and took the liberty of skimming his fingers along the edge of her hair.

"I know it and you know it," she said, shifting away from him, her heart tripping in her chest, her blood pumping through her veins. "And standing here talking to you isn't getting my work done."

He smiled a slow seductive smile that stopped her heart, then sent it speeding along even faster than before he had smiled at her. "Here I thought I was helping stimulate...your creative juices."

"I don't need your help. I don't want your help. I want to do this myself."

"Ah, yes, independent Alexis."

Pivoting away from him, she said, "It's not a crime."

"Isn't it?" he asked, catching her elbow and spinning her around again.

She ignored the tingle that raced up her arm just from the touch of his fingers on her skin. "I've never heard of anybody going to jail for being independent."

"No," he whispered, stepping close again. "But I'll bet you know a person who has lived her life in a sort of prison because she refused to let anyone inside."

For a minute she'd thought he was going to connect this whole conversation to Angus. Since he'd brought it directly back to her, she knew he was concerned, worried, about *her.* His presence here had nothing to do with her grandfather. He was here because he cared about her.

That knowledge filled her with warmth. She didn't have a clue what he was going to do now that he'd crossed the unofficial line, and subtly admitted that he cared about her. Gazing into his smoky amber eyes, she suspected he didn't have any idea, either. An unexpected juxtaposition occurred. Sexual and emotional feelings came face-to-face, then mixed and mingled. Lines of distinction blurred. A minute or two ticked off the clock with each of them quietly staring at the other, then, without warning, he bent his head and kissed her.

Where his first kiss had been potent, powerful, this kiss was soft, gentle, tender and exceedingly sweet, and in so being it was a hundred times more potent, more powerful, than the first. Though Alexis tried to fight it, the gentleness of it soothed her, even tamed her angry passion over her inability to create. As she raised her arms around his neck and felt his go around her waist, she found herself falling into the kiss by degrees, losing herself, losing her ability to think, to reason. Warmth coursed through her blood, her brain became pleasantly fogged. In his arms she felt safe, secure…things she hadn't felt in so long they frightened her.

Red-hot panic replaced sensual lethargy and she pushed him away. What was she doing kissing this man, accepting his help—thinking he cared for her, and feeling secure…? Actually the last was the problem. How could she feel secure with a man she hardly knew, except to recognize that being raised by Angus MacFarland had made Cal as undependable as Angus was?

"Why the hell do you keep doing that?" she asked, then swallowed the odd lump that had formed in her throat. Damn it! She *wanted* him to like her, and she wanted to like him. But it was foolish. He was too much like her grandfather. Flippant, frivolous, affectionate when it suited him. And distant to the point of abandonment when it didn't.

Stepping away from her, he drew a long breath. "Alexis, I know I shouldn't have kissed you. I'm sorry."

"You're sorry?" she asked quietly. "Do you have any idea what it does to me when you're nice to me one day and then pull away the next? You can't start adding kisses into the equation or I'll be totally crazy."

Cal rubbed his hand across the back of his neck. "I know. This is going to sound trite, but it's nothing personal, nothing against you."

For several seconds, Alexis only stared at him. She would have believed that if he'd been moody with Terry. He hadn't. He was consistently kind. Yet, she couldn't depend on him being nice to her from one day to the next. Finally she said, "I'm not buying it."

He looked as if he were going to bolt again, to leave her hanging, to refuse to explain, but after a short internal debate, he said, "I dated someone for a long, long time, the whole way through high school and a few years beyond. Thought I loved her," he said, then shrugged. "Probably I did."

"And she hurt you," Alexis surmised, irritated. One little broken heart and Cal turned against all women. This boy had to get out more.

"No, she didn't hurt me. I hurt her."

Chagrined, Alexis said, "Oh."

"I met another woman about six weeks before Cathy and I were supposed to be married. Becky just kind of blew into my life and took over. I called off the wedding, broke off my engagement and was in bed with Becky before sundown the same day."

Alexis stared at him incredulously. "You're kidding."

"I wish I were."

When he didn't say anything for several minutes, simply watched his fingers play across the worn wood of the desk, curiosity overcame Alexis and she said, "So what happened?"

"I bought her things, traveled with her, skipped out of the ranch work. In general, I spent six months glued to her side, living for the next time we'd make love."

Flabbergasted, Alexis crossed her arms on her chest and stared at him. It was impossible to picture this dyed-in-the-wool chauvinist putty in some woman's hands. If it weren't for her own conflicting feelings about him, she might have found this funny. "Go on."

"At the end of six months she dumped me."

"Just like that?" Alexis asked, snapping her fingers.

He met her eyes. "Just like that."

"What did you do?"

"Got drunk mostly. And when I got sober, really sober, I realized how much I'd hurt and humiliated Cathy. I realized that I'd deserted my sister. I realized I'd more or less abandoned Angus. In short, I realized what a fool I'd made of myself."

"Welcome to the club. Everybody's made a fool of himself at least once in his life."

"Not like this," Cal said, then ran his hands down his face. "Look, Alexis, I'm sorry. I guess the bottom line is I learned a lesson about myself. I completely lost control and I don't want to go through that again. That's why I'm very cautious about getting involved."

"I don't blame you," Alexis said softly, then made her way to the chair behind the desk. "If you'll excuse me, I have work to do."

Cal didn't make any further argument or explanation; he simply left the room. When he was gone, Alexis sunk into the comfort of the old leather chair, pressing her fingertips to her eyelids. In a sense she knew she'd dodged a bullet because she didn't want to get involved with a man who still hadn't worked out the problems of his last relationship. But in another sense she felt bereft. Another place, another time, she and Cal might have been very, very good together. As it was, she had no choice but to stay the hell away from him.

She couldn't settle for second best. She could not be number two in a man's life. Hell, she hadn't yet been number one in *anyone's* life. When it came to sex, settling down and forever, she was making damned sure the man she chose didn't have a heartbreak and a cloud of guilt that would hold the best part of him an arm's distance from her.

Chapter Eight

"Alexis, your mother's on the phone."

Sitting under the umbrella-covered redwood table, Alexis peered up from the draft copy she was reading. Cal stood in the opening for the sliding glass door, looking both ruggedly handsome and yet somehow domesticated with Terry stuck to his hip. Though Terry wore bright plaid shorts and Cal's long, lean legs were encased in denim, both wore white T-shirts. But where Terry's was "little-boy" loose, Cal's tightly hugged his well-muscled chest.

Noticing Cal's long legs first, then the blastedly snug fit of his shirt caused Alexis's pulse to scramble. She hadn't forgotten what he'd told her the night before. She simply didn't know how to treat Cal, and she was even less sure of how to curb her own emotions. No one ever made her feel the way Cal did when he kissed her. Not because of the tingles, the excitement or even the instant arousal. The security, the comfort level was what she didn't understand. A rational woman couldn't feel secure with a man who wouldn't commit—and that was the real bottom line to his explanation. He might find her sexually attractive, he might even like her, but there was no way he would ever commit himself again.

"My mother?" she said, bringing herself back to the much safer present. She was astounded that her mother had called the ranch, but it was also odd that Cal didn't seem put off about speaking with Angus's wayward daughter as Alexis thought he might have been.

She took the portable phone from Cal's hands. "Mom?"

"How are you, dear?"

"Well, I'm fine," Alexis said cheerfully, still so astonished by her mother's call that she hadn't yet figured out there must be a reason for it. When she did make that connection, she felt all the blood drain from her face. "How are *you?* Is something wrong?" she asked in a rush.

Her mother laughed. "No. Nothing's wrong. I was worried about you. You couldn't hide your concern for Terry yesterday and, frankly, it troubled me. I need to hear that you're okay."

"Yeah, I'm fine," Alexis said pragmatically, then she sighed. "Unless you count the fact that I haven't had an actual productive day in a week and I'm working toward a deadline with the new *Diet Splash* campaign."

"What's the problem?"

"I have an idea. I know I have an idea. I just can't seem to stimulate it into making itself known."

"Writer's block?"

"No, this is worse. It's like my subconscious has already figured out the whole campaign and the idea is sitting on the edge of my brain. But I can't push the right button to have the actual thought, and my subconscious is laughing at me."

"You're working too hard," Rachel said, chuckling.

With everything that had happened to her lately, Alexis couldn't have agreed more. Even forgetting her feelings for Cal, her life was a mess. "That's exactly what I think. I was up until four o'clock this morning, doing everything from free-fall writing to handstands, trying to nudge the idea loose and nothing helped. Then, at five-thirty, regular as clockwork, Terry knocked at my door. I took him downstairs, made him breakfast, played hangman, took him to the barn…''

"You're working too hard," her mother repeated, this time emphatically.

"I have to," Alexis insisted.

"No, you don't. Take a rest. Take a break. For goodness' sake, just get one good night's sleep.''

"I'll sleep when this campaign is solid.''

Alexis's mother clicked her tongue in annoyance. "If you don't soon sleep the campaign may never get solid.''

"You're making it sound like I'm chasing my tail.''

"I think you are.''

"Yeah, well, at this point I don't have much choice. If I don't soon earn our retainer, even that will go away,'' Alexis said, though she hated reminding her mother of the obvious. If Alexis didn't bring the business back financially, her mother would lose the one thing she'd accomplished in her life.

"The company doesn't mean that much to me.''

Alexis's face scrunched in bewilderment. "That's part of the problem. It *should* mean much more to you than it does.''

"I have a lovely home, financial security and a beautiful daughter. As far as I'm concerned, one little drop in the bucket business I created to entertain myself while Garret was away is the absolute least of my worries.''

Alexis would have felt much better if she believed her mother was only saying that to protect her feelings. But Alexis knew her mother genuinely felt that way. The spark was gone. Her fires had all died out. And the one link she had with passion, Alexis had destroyed.

"Then it looks like I really do have my work cut out for me because as long as you're indifferent, I have to put the company back together again, if only so you have *something*.''

Though Alexis had been trying to push her mother, to make her mad, Rachel laughed. ''Now, you're talking nonsense. I swear you think I'm a poverty-stricken bag lady.''

''And I'd swear you think I'm an imbecilic child who can't see what's going on around her,'' Alexis retorted, tired and borderline angry because her mother just wouldn't fight back anymore. ''If you can't give me credit for wanting to return what I took from you, then at least give me credit for being mature enough to see there's a problem in your life. It shames me that we're not close enough that you'll tell me.''

Because she was exhausted, half-crazed from too much work and too little sleep, confused about what was happening to her with Cal and guilt ridden about ruining her mother's business, Alexis disconnected the phone call without giving her mother a chance to comment. When she looked up, Cal was staring at her.

''Don't you think you were a little hard on her?''

''And what the hell would you know and what the hell would you care?'' Alexis said in exasperation, as she rose from the redwood table. ''As far as you're concerned, my mother and I are nothing but thorns in your side.''

When she turned to walk away, Cal caught her wrist and hauled her back. ''From what I understood from your end of the conversation, it sounded to me like she was trying to let you off the hook.''

Alexis shook Cal's hand off her wrist with one swift swipe. ''I don't want off the hook! Can't you see that?'' She stopped, raised her face to the heavens and heaved a frustrated sigh. ''Can't anybody see that? Am I the only person who realizes how much trouble my mother is in?''

Cal held her gaze for a few seconds. ''I don't know. *Are* you the only person who sees how much trouble your mother is in?''

"Obviously, yes."

"Then maybe you'd better think about that. If no one else sees this trouble, are you sure there is trouble?"

Alexis looked him right in the eye. "Yes. Yes, I am sure there is trouble. If I wasn't sure, I wouldn't be here. And just thinking back to the things I told you the day I came here, you have to know it, too. Because I wouldn't have come to this godforsaken ranch, Mr. Wright, if I would have had any other choice. Now, if you'll excuse me."

She left him standing in the middle of the patio, the warm midmorning sun beating on his back. Because he had the sneaking suspicion she was going up to her room, and would probably fall asleep if she'd just let herself lie on the bed, Cal followed her into the kitchen, then continued to stalk her, staying several feet behind her until he heard her bedroom door slam. Hoping the bed would tempt her as long as no other distraction diverted her, Cal found Terry and hustled him outside.

"We have to be quiet so Alexis can get some sleep," he told the little boy as they walked out onto the patio.

"What're we gonna do?" Terry asked Cal, squinting up at him.

"Once we get you out of those sissy shorts, we could ride," Cal suggested.

"Okay!" Terry enthusiastically agreed as the portable phone on the table rang.

Because Cal knew the portable was typically one ring behind the other phones, he recognized that Alexis might have already heard the first ring and be on her way to answer it…and he didn't want her to do that. He wanted her to go to sleep. He hadn't meant to kiss her the night before, or to tell her his life story, or to make her feel rejected, but he knew he had. Just as she seemed to do with everybody else and everything else in her life, she had taken the blame, though this was his problem, not hers. He couldn't explain that to her while she was so edgy, but after she got some sleep he would talk some sense into her.

In one swift grab, he scooped the phone off the table and said, "Hello, Triple Moors."

"Well, hello again."

Uncomfortable, Cal said, "Hello, Mrs. Elliott."

"Since it appears I'm going to be calling for my daughter regularly, you and I should at least dispense with formalities. You may call me Rachel."

"Rachel," Cal agreed, nodding awkwardly. He'd heard so much about this soft-spoken women, none of it bad, per se, just more or less damning, that he never expected her voice to be warm like a smile. He never expected to have feelings about her...except maybe dislike. Yet, by actually talking with her he was reconsidering all his preconceived notions.

"May I speak with my daughter again?"

"Actually, Mrs....Rachel. She just stormed upstairs and Terry and I are hoping she'll flop on the bed in anger, stay down in frustration and fall asleep from exhaustion long enough that when she wakes up she'll only be as dangerous as a rattler. We can handle rattlers."

Angling beside Cal, Terry laughed. Through the phone lines, Rachel laughed. Cal didn't think he'd been funny.

"I see your point. Tell her I called, and that I'll call again."

"I could have her call you," Cal volunteered carefully.

"That would be wonderful. I'm so worried, and not just because she hung up on me. Since the business took a turn for the worse, Alexis has been too hard on herself. She shouldn't be. The business she feels she's losing isn't our bread and butter. It was my hobby for fifteen years until she became president and made it into something unexpected. But instead of taking this setback in stride, learning from her mistakes and moving on, she's obsessed with saving it." Rachel paused to sigh. "Though I admire her passion, I don't understand it. But I do know one thing. I won't let her work herself to death for something as foolish as money.''

Cal couldn't have agreed more, until the word ''passion'' registered in his brain and he had the profound thought that Alexis felt about her advertising company the way he felt about the Triple Moors. He knew instinctively that it was nothing so simple as money that kept her working as much or as hard as she did.

''I don't think you're going to be able to stop her.''

There was a smile in Rachel Elliott's voice when she said, ''You haven't seen me in action. I haven't forced an issue in quite a few years, but I have a feeling my temper won't be a hard thing to resurrect.''

Because he believed it, Cal grinned. ''So, I guess this means we'll be seeing you.''

''Yes,'' Rachel said, suddenly sounding incredibly strong and sure of herself. ''Yes. If I remember correctly, Alexis said she still had a week or so before she had to make any decisions. So, yes, if I can't get her to listen to reason within the next day or two I think you just might be seeing me.''

Cal laughed and disconnected the call. But before his hand had pulled away from the portable, he stopped dead.

He'd just royally blown Angus's plan. He'd just talked Rachel into visiting the ranch about a week too soon.

''So, just give your mother a call,'' Cal suggested casually as he peeled potatoes, Alexis seasoned hamburgers and Terry rolled a toy truck across the scarred kitchen table. In light of his bigger problem, he'd completely forgotten his plan to tell her his decision to stay away from her had nothing to do with her and everything to do with him. ''See what she wanted when she called back.''

''She talked to you,'' Alexis said accusingly.

Uncertain of why that might be bad, Cal shrugged. ''A little.''

"She made you think I was crazy."

"Your mother doesn't think you're crazy. She thinks you're tired."

"I was tired. I took a nap. I'm not tired anymore. And I still think there's something wrong."

"Alexis, your mother doesn't think there is anything wrong with her life. She sounds perfectly happy and perfectly delightful."

"Oh, so now *you* think I'm crazy."

"No, I do not think you're crazy," Cal emphatically denied, feeling as if he'd sunk to his knees in quicksand and getting the fatal realization that he wasn't coming out. "I think you're passionate and spirited about your business, which is good. Great actually. It hit me today that you probably feel the same way about Elliott-MacFarland Advertising as I feel about this ranch. So I understand your die-hard determination to save it and I even applaud you."

Thinking that should have gotten him at least back to only calf-deep in quicksand, Cal was completely unprepared when Alexis marched over to the sink where he stood, put her fists on her hips and said, "But?"

"But nothing," Cal assured her. "I think all that is great."

"But?" Alexis demanded again.

"But nothing," Cal insisted, trying desperately to be convincing. All Alexis had to do was call Rachel and talk like a normal, rational, happy woman and Rachel would delay her travel plans. But he knew Alexis wouldn't call, wouldn't sound happy and wouldn't cause her mother to delay her plans if she heard Cal's "but."

Hands planted on her hips, Alexis said, "There is a but in there. And if you don't tell me what it is, I will definitely assume you think I'm crazy. Otherwise, you wouldn't consider me incapable of dealing with bad news."

Cal sighed. God, when this woman got insistent, she went straight for the jugular. "All right. You want to know what the but is? I'll tell you what the but is. I admire your spunk, your courage, your determination to put your business back together again. But...but,'' he repeated loudly, if only to irritate her because God knew she had a way of getting to him, ''I think you're here more to buy yourself some time than to save your mother.''

For a good thirty seconds, Alexis only stared at him. Then her expression shifted into one of complete confusion, and she said, ''That's bull.''

Because she walked away, Cal turned from the sink, leaned against it and crossed his arms on his chest. ''Really? You think so? Well, I don't.''

''If you're trying to get me to argue with you, save your breath. I'm not going to rebut something that doesn't make any sense.''

''But it does make sense. You're afraid you don't have the answers to your work questions. You don't know why your business fell apart. You don't know how to get it back together again. You don't even have a good idea for the one client who continues to retain you out of loyalty for the fabulous campaign you did for him last year. So rather than panic, you focused your attention on your mother and now you have an excuse. I can't think myself out of this mess because I'm preoccupied. Oh, and by the way, you're also hampering yourself by being at a ranch. Thousands of miles away from the hub of your business, but you didn't run. Not even to buy yourself a little time. You're here to save your mother.''

Openmouthed, Alexis stared at him. ''You cretin.''

''No,'' Cal said, shaking his head. ''You're not going to get away with that. You asked for what I thought. Demanded I tell you what I thought. Now, you deal with it.''

''You mean deal with it like you dealt with your problems after your girlfriend dumped you?''

Realizing she was only striking back out of anger or hurt, Cal calmly said, ''The situations are entirely different.''

"How?" she asked pleasantly.

Cal's eyes narrowed. "They just are. One is a personal thing the other is a business thing. Besides, you haven't made a fool of yourself."

"And you're trying to tell me you're not evading your issues? It's easy to throw around vague terms like 'made a fool of yourself' and not ever completely define the problem. As far as I'm concerned, that just means you won't face it."

Dumbfounded, he stared at her. "What do you mean, I won't face it? Lady, I faced it. I had to come home and listen to jeers from the hands and be the object of gossip from the good ladies at church. *I faced it.*"

"Oh sure, you faced the easy stuff. But you won't face the hard stuff like trying again. At least I have the courage to stay in the game. You bailed out. You won't even try."

He pierced her with a look. "Actually I probably would try again—with the right woman. But so far, I haven't felt anything more than a sexual attraction for anybody. With as cheap as sex comes these days, I don't think pursuing that's worth the effort."

With that he strode to the table, picked up the newly shaped hamburgers and started out to the grill. When he was gone, Alexis collapsed against the sink. She knew that comment wouldn't have stung so much if she hadn't asked for it.

Or if she didn't find him so blastedly perfect. He probably would have never found the need to come right out and say he was only sexually attracted to her if she hadn't pushed him.

Chapter Nine

Hearing a knock on the front door, Alexis ran down the circular stairway of the foyer. "I'm coming," she called, knowing full well the visitor wouldn't hear her, but fulfilling a politeness ingrained in her from the age of two. But before she got to the bottom of the steps, Ryan Kelly let himself in.

Hat in his hand, he grinned at her. "Sorry."

"Oh, you don't have to be sorry. Cal explained that this had been your home. I'd feel like a real heel if you thought you had to knock because of me."

"Thanks."

"Cal's out in the barn," she said cheerfully, and more or less pointed him in that direction.

"Actually I need to speak with both of you. I found Terry's aunt. I called her house, but there was no one home, so I left a message on an answering machine."

Alexis hardly registered anything Ryan said after the part about finding Terry's aunt. Her heart had swelled in her chest and it was difficult to breathe. Realizing she had no right to interfere, and probably no right to even voice her concerns, Alexis only cleared her throat. "I'll get Cal."

Ryan shook his head. "I'll get Cal. You bring some iced tea to the patio and we'll strategize."

Assuming he was merely trying to make her feel better, Alexis smiled ruefully. "I didn't think we had any options."

"Well, we're also not going to hand Terry off to the first person who comes along. Let me go get Cal," he said reassuringly. "Then we'll hash all this out together."

By the time Cal and Ryan returned from the barn, Alexis had the tea on the patio table. She recognized that it had taken them a little longer than she expected to get to the house, but she wasn't even going to consider that they might have made decisions without her. If she did, she'd get angry again and she didn't want to be angry. She wanted her nice, safe, normal life back, where everything made sense.

Unfortunately she knew she wasn't going to get it. And she also wasn't going to let them make this decision without her.

"Thanks, Alexis," Ryan said as he took a seat at the table and poured himself a glass of tea.

"You and Cal weren't by any chance discussing this situation without me?" she asked immediately, not letting them have an opportunity to think they might have fooled her.

Ryan laughed, but Cal cursed. "Can't you let anything get by you?" he demanded.

"I don't want to be left out of decisions that affect me."

"Well, even though this decision doesn't affect you directly, Miss Smarty-Pants, we didn't discuss any part of it because we *want* your opinion."

Alexis gaped at Cal. "Really? You *want* my opinion."

"You are a woman," Ryan said, chagrined. "And Cal and I don't have much in the way of gentler sensibilities. We always depended on Cal's sister, Grace, to help us."

"Especially at Christmastime," Cal interjected.

"Especially with *women*," Ryan contradicted, then sipped his tea.

Cal wasn't sure why but that last comment bothered him. Why Ryan felt the need to subtly inform Alexis that the two of them were complete dunderheads around the opposite sex, Cal didn't know, but he did feel Ryan had sent out a signal. And he also felt Ryan had done it deliberately.

Luckily Alexis either didn't hear or chose to ignore Ryan's last statement. "So, what do we do about Terry?" she asked.

"I haven't figured that out," Ryan answered honestly. "I thought the three of us could discuss parameters. Like, if this is the right Maria Jenkins, should we investigate her financial situation before we let her take Terry? Should we check to see if she has a criminal record? Or should we take the position that since she's a blood relative, Terry should live with her no matter what her situation? That is, if she wants him."

Alexis's breath hissed out. *"If she wants him?"*

"I realize it seems heartless," Ryan said. "But usually an analysis has to be. Because the truth is we don't have a clue what we're going to find. We could investigate and discover Maria Jenkins has got money galore, but she has no interest in Terry. Or we could discover she's dirt poor but a wonderful woman who would make a fabulous mother. So, we have to consider all our options."

"I can't believe anyone would turn Terry away."

"Believe me, Alexis," Ryan said, "I've seen worse. But, as far as Terry is concerned, no matter what we find out about Maria Jenkins through investigation, my vote is that we're going to have to reserve judgment until we meet her."

"In other words, you're proposing that we more or less insist she come to us," Alexis said delightedly.

Ryan inclined his head in agreement. "We'll explain she needs to come here to pick up Terry and Bertha. It's not an unreasonable request since Bertha will just be getting out of the hospital and won't be able to take public transportation to New Mexico. That way, when Maria comes here, we'll all have a chance to get a look at her, and see what we think.''

''I agree,'' Cal said when he saw the ridiculous spark of hope in Alexis's eyes at the idea of getting to meet Terry's prospective guardian. He understood and appreciated that as long as Alexis could see Terry was going to someone capable, she would be able to let him go. Because, Cal sensed, part of her fear stemmed from feeling helpless. In the short time he'd known her, Cal had seen she hated to be helpless.

''Then it's more or less settled,'' Alexis said.

Though she said it happily, obviously convinced they were doing the right thing, Cal noticed that she was twisting her hands, which she had bunched on her lap, and he got a pang of compassion. She was nervous for Terry because she knew firsthand what it was like to go into a strange home.

But, then again, so did he.

''The move from my family home into Angus's home was actually a blessing,'' Cal quietly told Alexis, then watched as she deliberately stilled her hands, as if she surmised that her nervous gesture had alerted Cal to her need for comfort. He nearly laid his hand on hers, if only in a show of support, but he stopped himself. Enough bad feelings had passed between them to last a lifetime. He couldn't overstep any more boundaries. He always ended up in trouble.

''My move into Angus's home was the best thing that could have happened to me, too,'' Ryan said. Grinning foolishly, he nodded to Cal. ''I got something my parents never gave me—a brother. If Terry's aunt has kids, it will be a treat for him to have someone to fight with.''

''I suppose,'' Alexis agreed softly.

Hearing the anguish in her voice, Cal's heart splintered and again he got that overpowering need to comfort her. No matter what they told her, this wasn't going to be easy for her. Unlike Ryan and Cal, Alexis hadn't gone into a home with kids her own age and a happy, supportive family. She'd gone into a home filled with impatient adults, most of whom thought she was a nuisance.

"It's not going to be like that," Cal assured her, and this time he did lay his hand on hers. He saw Ryan raise his eyebrows in question but he ignored him because he understood why Alexis's pain troubled him so much. If it weren't for Angus, Cal would probably feel uneasy about Terry, too. Gratitude to Angus—and maybe even guilt that Alexis should have had Cal's share of Angus's love—compelled him to comfort her. He wasn't overstepping any boundaries or butting in where he didn't belong. He was doing what needed to be done. There was no more to it than that.

"Well, I guess I'll be on my way," Ryan said and pushed his chair away from the table so he could stand. "I'll call the minute I hear anything."

When Ryan left, Cal squeezed Alexis's hand. "I recognize things didn't work out for you once you left the Triple Moors, but we don't know yet what Terry's situation is going to be. And I think rather than worrying about it, we should give this aunt of his the benefit of the doubt and hope for the best."

Alexis gave him a ghost of a smile. "I do have a tendency to worry about things."

"My God, woman, you certainly do," Cal agreed, glad that her mood appeared to be getting back to normal. Even forgetting the sexual attraction, Cal wasn't sure how much more he could handle of this—the drama of Angus, the drama of Alexis's mother, the drama of Terry—but one thing was certain. If Oprah called, he would be ready.

"I'm going out to the stables now," Cal said, rising from his chair. "I'm going to find myself a particularly wicked horse and I'm not coming back until he's broken."

Alexis smiled up at him. "You wouldn't happen to have two horses like that?"

"Yes, but I'm not letting you near either one of them. Fifteen seconds of making friends and you'd be campaigning to free all my horses rather than break them, and then I'd be up the creek without a paddle." He started to leave, but paused, turned back and cupped her chin in his palm. "Your heart's too soft," he said, then walked away.

But Alexis sat back on her chair, thinking the pot had just officially called the kettle black. Cal didn't even like her, but he'd comforted her...in front of his brother. He'd completely forgotten his own feelings and his reputation of being a tough guy because he couldn't stand to see her misery.

That didn't merely surprise her, it warmed her all over, charmed her when she didn't want to be charmed—couldn't afford to be charmed—because he'd told her, blatantly, straight out told her, he felt nothing but sexual attraction for her.

If she let him charm her enough, she'd forget that, and then she'd be the one who was hurt.

They didn't have to wait long the following morning for Ryan's call. In fact, when Ryan phoned, it was to announce that Terry's aunt had driven all night to get to Crossroads Creek. Her plan was to check on her mother's condition by going to the hospital, but first she wanted to see Terry.

For Alexis, the twenty minutes it took Ryan to get Maria from the sheriff's office to the ranch were interminable. She alternated between thinking she was projecting too much of her own anxiety on Terry and thinking that they were all crazy for even considering giving a child they loved to a stranger. But the minute the door of the police cruiser opened and Maria stepped out, Terry lit up like a sparkler on the Fourth of July.

"Aunt Mimi!" he said and bounded toward her.

"Terry!" she said, stooping to catch him as he ran to her. From what Cal could tell she was a younger version of Bertha. Short, a little chubby and very, very easygoing.

When Terry landed in her arms, he began to sob. Cal and Alexis exchanged a look of alarm. But Ryan sidled up to them and said, "Maria told me in the car that when Terry was a baby she had lived with him and his mother. I didn't prompt or prod, and she began telling stories of how she baby-sat Terry, the Christmases they'd spent together and even recent visits at Bertha's."

Ryan paused, drew a cautious breath. "Not only does Terry know his aunt, but it sounds like he's going to extremely capable hands."

"Yes, I see that," Alexis agreed cheerfully. "And I'm very relieved," she added sincerely. Smiling brightly, she walked over to Maria and Terry and hunkered beside them, soothing Terry and joining in on their conversation.

"There, see," Ryan said, pointing in the direction of the endearing scene. "There's nothing to worry about."

"So it seems," Cal agreed, because he wished it were true. He wished it so much that he decided that if Alexis had chosen to act as if she was unaffected by Terry's leaving, then he was going to let her.

"It was nice of you to invite Maria for dinner," Cal said as he and Alexis worked to prepare the evening meal.

"She's tired from her trip, worried about her mother and excited about bringing Terry back into her life all at the same time," Alexis said with a laugh. "The woman is going through so many emotions, I didn't think she needed the stress of cooking added to her life."

"And it should also be a good transition for Terry," Cal agreed casually as he washed lettuce, but before he could finish his thought there was a knock at the back door and his sister, Grace, entered without being invited.

"Hello..." she singsonged, opening her arms to Cal.

"Well, hello to you, stranger," Cal said both pleasure and surprise evident in his voice. "Alexis," he said, after accepting his sister's quick hug. "This is my sister, Grace."

Because his attention had been diverted by the situation with Terry, Cal had forgotten that for Alexis Grace was more like the enemy than either he or Ryan. Grace had been adopted by Angus. Legally she was Alexis's aunt.

"How do you do?" Alexis said carefully.

"Fine, thank you. It's a pleasure to meet you," Grace said, studying Alexis.

In many ways the two women were similar and could have actually been mistaken for relatives. Though Grace's hair wasn't as black as Alexis's, it was every bit as thick and the styles were similar. Alexis's eyes were pale green, and Grace's eyes were pale blue. Mysterious. Intriguing. And full of questions. Each woman was intensely curious about the other.

But rather than say anything, both seemed to choose to avoid or ignore the questions that hummed between them.

"Can you join us for dinner?" Alexis asked politely as Grace walked to the round maple wood table.

Grace grimaced. "I promised Madison and Ryan I'd have dinner with them. I'm here because I needed to discuss something with Cal."

"You never come to me for advice, or need anything from me except when you…" *Want me to hide something from Angus.* He almost said it, then clamped his mouth shut. There were enough problems between these two already. He didn't want to add fuel to the fire.

Luckily Grace didn't notice that he'd paused midsentence. She batted a dismissing hand. "It's nothing like my usual things. This is actually good news," she began, but her eyes also filled with tears.

Cal honest to God thought his heart stopped. He cursed the fact that there were now two women in his life where previously there had been none, and dashed over to crouch beside Grace when she fell to a seat by the table. "What's wrong?" he asked frantically.

"Oh, Cal, nothing's wrong," she said tearfully. "I'm excited and weepy and weird—emotionally weird—because I'm pregnant."

Cal almost fainted. "What?" he whispered incredulously.

"I'm pregnant."

"But you just…"

Grace laughed heartily. "I've been married for ten years."

"Yeah, right," Cal said, not at all amused that she could so flippantly refer to the fact that she'd been secretly married for ten years and estranged from her husband. He still wasn't a hundred percent sure he'd adjusted to that situation. "You're pregnant," he said, realizing suddenly that his baby sister was going to have a baby. "Pregnant," he repeated, then touched his fingertips to her face. He almost couldn't believe it.

Neither could Alexis. It dawned on her suddenly that coming down here she'd not only opened herself up to the possibility that she'd have to face her grandfather, but she'd opened herself up to his entire life. She was tending to his neighbor boy. She'd cleaned his house. And seeing Cal's reaction to his sister's pregnancy, it suddenly became crystal clear that she didn't just like Cal and what she felt for him was nothing as simple as sexual attraction. She was falling in love with Angus's right-hand man, a man who wanted absolutely nothing to do with her.

It was all happening so fast she felt as if she didn't have any control over it.

Right then and there she knew she had to get out of the kitchen. Since Cal and his sister were still engrossed in each other she didn't even feel the need to excuse herself. Instead she slipped her apron over her head and directed herself toward the car keys.

How could she possibly let herself fall in love with a man who didn't want her? Hadn't she had enough rejection to last her a lifetime?

Chapter Ten

When Terry got ready to leave the following afternoon, Alexis promised herself she wouldn't cry because worrying too much about Terry was the first area in which she had to get control. Terry was going into a good home with a woman who not only wanted to care for the little boy but also for Terry's grandmother, so there was nothing to worry about. Terry's station in life had actually taken a turn for the better.

Maria arrived in an older model, midsize car, but Alexis immediately noticed it was clean and well tended. Ryan was behind her in the police cruiser. They got out of their vehicles simultaneously, then walked to the porch where Cal, Terry and Alexis waited for them.

Maria took Alexis's hand. "Thank you very much for caring for Terry through this."

Alexis smiled. "It was my pleasure. He's quite a character."

"Yes, he is," Maria agreed, gazing fondly at the little boy who had positioned himself at her side.

It was easy for Alexis to see that Terry was genuinely

happy, and extremely comfortable with his new situation. And though Alexis was sorry to see him go, she knew this was the right thing for him.

She swallowed the lump that formed in her throat and stooped beside him. "You be good for Maria and your grandma, okay?" she said softly, then ruffled his straight brown hair.

Terry looked at the ground. "Okay," he agreed gruffly.

"You're not gonna cry on me, are you?" Alexis asked, lifting Terry's chin so she could see his face. His lips were trembling. "Hey, hey," she said, then gathered him into her arms. He threw his arms around her neck and squeezed tightly. Alexis closed her eyes. She wasn't going to cry. She wasn't. This was for the best. From the looks of things, Terry was entering a much better home than the one he'd started off with.

"I'm really going to miss you," she whispered to the little boy who had wrapped himself around her. Then she drew back so she could look into his eyes. "But I'm also very happy for you. Your Aunt Maria is a very nice person, and you'll still be with your grandma. All in all, you got a pretty good deal."

Terry sniffed, then nodded.

"And that doesn't mean I won't miss you or that we won't see each other again." She paused, tilted her head as if thinking. "Tell you what. How about if Cal and I make arrangements to have you visit the ranch next summer for a few weeks?"

Terry immediately brightened. "Can I?"

"Sure," Alexis answered, then looked up at Cal who was watching her carefully. "We could have Terry spend a week with us next year, right?" she asked Cal.

"Absolutely," he agreed, reaching down and boosting Terry into his arms. "We'll finish those riding lessons."

"Okay," Terry said, then gave Cal a squeeze.

"Okay," Cal said, returning Terry's hug before he slid him to the ground again.

"Well, we'd better get going," Maria said. "I left Mom at the house. She wanted to call a friend or two to give out her new address and phone, then we'll be on our way."

Alexis ruffled Terry's hair again. "You be good, okay?"

Terry nodded.

"And we'll see you next year," Cal reminded optimistically.

Terry nodded again.

Apparently recognizing that neither Alexis, nor Cal, nor Terry could quite say that final goodbye, Maria began leading Terry to the car. "I'll make sure that he drops you a note now and again."

Her stiff smile in place, Alexis nodded. Cal put his arm around her shoulders and though Alexis longed to step into its familiar warmth, she shifted away. She didn't want his comfort. She didn't want anybody's comfort. She didn't *need* anybody's comfort. Least of all his.

"Well, I guess it's time for me to head into the office and see if I can come up with something snappy," she said brightly and walked away from Cal and Ryan who stood staring at Maria's car as it disappeared on the horizon.

"Don't you think you ought to take this afternoon off?" Cal called after her.

She turned and forced a smile. "No. I took enough time off. I think my body and mind need to be whipped into a creative frenzy."

With that she pivoted and jogged up the three steps into the house.

"Don't even try picturing that," Cal cautioned Ryan who was staring blankly at the closed door of the ranch house. "I walked in on her the other night and she was all but shooting sparks out of her ears. Creativity is frightening."

"Tell me about it," Ryan said, reminding Cal that Madison was a woman driven by creativity, too. Then he sighed and said, "Well, at least Alexis didn't take Terry's leaving too hard."

"Actually she took it too well."

"Nah," Ryan said, dismissing Cal's concern. "She's fine. Once someone's ready to go back to work, the worst is over."

"I'd agree if she'd only started acting weird like this today. But even before Grace left the house last night I noticed a difference in her."

Though he didn't think it was possible. He'd been so preoccupied with the fact that he was about to become an uncle—for real—and with the fact that he'd actually be getting another genuine relative, that it floored him. Then Maria and Terry arrived for dinner about two minutes before Alexis returned home. But since Cal didn't know where Alexis was or when she'd be returning, he had to rush to finish the preparations for their meal. Noticing that Alexis had returned behaving like a stranger was too odd to be true. As distracted as he was, even seeing Alexis in the room should have been a miracle. Instead he'd not only seen her, but he'd also clearly seen the change.

"You think her turnaround might have something to do with Grace's being pregnant?"

Cal shook his head. "I don't know. I can't get a handle on her anymore. She's supposed to hate her grandfather, but she's so softhearted I can't imagine her hating anyone. She's trying to save her mother, but I can't see that her mother needs saving. She's supposed to be some kind of whiz kid, but even though she's got every piece of office equipment known to mankind sitting in Angus's study, I haven't seen her turn out any work."

"You want me to have Madison come by this afternoon to talk with her?"

Cal thought about it, then dismissed it. "No," he said firmly. "The only thing I'm really sure about with Alexis is that she's a private person. If she thinks Madison came here to give her help or moral support, or even just a shoulder to cry on, she'll suspect you and I had something to do with it. And it will make her mad that we're interfering.''

"Okay," Ryan agreed reluctantly. "But just remember if you need me…or Madison, we're only a phone call away."

"Yeah, right, okay," Cal said distractedly, his gaze drifting over to the house.

Ryan headed for his cruiser. Before he pulled open the door, he looked as if he might say something else, but in the last second he changed his mind. But Cal didn't care. He was about as preoccupied as he could be with the woman in his den and though he usually didn't cotton to being confounded by a woman, this time it was different. He didn't feel an out-of-control need to please her. He didn't feel she was the end-all, be-all to his happiness. No, what he felt was good old compassion, or maybe understanding because everything that happened to her since she'd returned to the Triple Moors was negative.

So, if Cal wanted to help her, it didn't mean he was in love with her. If he wanted to entertain her, give her an evening of relaxation so she'd forget her troubles and maybe get her creativity back, then he wasn't smitten, or lovesick, or even infatuated. He was being a friend, a Good Samaritan. Nothing more.

Besides, he'd already laid it on the line that he wasn't interested and she'd understood. Not only was there no turning back from that opinion for him, but he was certain there'd be no misinterpretation by her if he did something nice for her.

"You did what?"

"I packed a picnic."

She stared at him. "A picnic *supper?*"

"Sure," he said, shrugging. "Why not?"

"I just always thought picnics were a lunch thing."

"Oh, you city people," Cal said, hoisting the basket from

the table. "You're so sure everything has to be a certain way."

Relaxing a little, Alexis flexed her neck. "I think that's because things go much smoother, or maybe it helps us get along in a crowded city, if we all believe we're playing by the same rules."

"Is that why you make those rules so tight and rigid?" Cal asked, grinning.

"The tighter the rules, the more rigid the rules…" Alexis began.

"The more chance you can make yourself crazy trying to live by them," Cal suggested, then took her elbow and directed her out the kitchen door and to his Jeep, which waited just beyond the patio.

Because the top was off the Jeep and a steady stream of air provided a constant buzz around them, they drove across the fields and meadows without saying anything. Because Cal was being so cavalier about the picnic—particularly the fact that it was a kind gesture—Alexis decided to adopt his attitude. This was a nothing—"meant nothing"—kind of a gesture. It was a "we-have-to-eat-anyway-so-let's-have-a-picnic-since-it's-such-a-nice-day" kind of thing. She could see that from the way he was behaving. If he wanted her to think it was something more, he'd be solicitous. If he felt she needed cheering up because of Terry, he'd be sweeter. As it was, he took her to a nice shady spot, and he provided food, but he was neither romantic, nor sweet. He was absolutely normal.

Thank God.

Taking a seat on the blanket he provided, Alexis tucked her legs beneath her and began removing utensils from the basket. "So what are we eating?"

"Well, I cheated. I went to the diner and bought fried chicken."

She eyed him suspiciously. "Real fried chicken."

"Don't tell me you're afraid of a little cholesterol?"

"Absolutely not. Especially not after four hours of pouring my heart and soul onto paper and still not creating a damned thing."

"I can't imagine how you do it."

"Do what?"

"Create," Cal said simply. "When I wake up in the morning, I know exactly what I have to do, where I have to do it and how it should be done. Not only that but I know I have the skills to do what needs done because I've been doing this kind of work for fifteen years. You, on the other hand, might have the skills—you can write, you can type, you might even be able to draw—but creating isn't like typing. You can't sit down and say since I can type a hundred words a minute I should be able to have ten pages of text in an hour, like I can say 'this afternoon I'm going to mend fences.' If you don't get an idea or inspiration, you're sunk. You can actually spend the entire day typing and not get anything done."

"That's how I spent this afternoon," Alexis confessed, toasting him with her can of cola.

"You didn't get *anything* done?" Cal asked sympathetically.

"No, actually, I did get something done. I beat myself up enough that I finally got the concept."

"So you're moving along?"

"No, now I have a starting place. But I should be moving along tomorrow," Alexis reported with a laugh.

"That's great."

A companionable silence descended over them as Cal happily devoured his share of dinner and Alexis realized he *had* brought her out here to cheer her up.

She supposed there were worse things in life, then she mentally grimaced. Who was she trying to kid? The fact that he liked her enough to do something so considerate filled her with warmth. She loved him. And whether he wanted to admit it or not, he had feelings for her, too. Real, genuine, solid feelings. Feelings enough that he'd do something sweet for her.

The only problem was, she had no idea what to do about it. She recognized that he'd told her about his last relationship to keep things simple between them and she also knew he was so sure it was working that he was letting his guard down. If she pushed him, he'd bolt, but if she didn't push him, he'd never admit the truth.

"Hear from your mother today?" he asked casually.

Alexis looked up. "No. Did you?"

Cal laughed. "No. And don't let Ryan hear you ask that. He already thinks I'm far too involved in Angus's business. He hasn't said anything but I've known him long enough that I can see the suspicion in his eyes."

"That's funny."

"What?"

"That you and Ryan have known each other long enough and well enough that he doesn't even have to tell you he thinks you're interfering, you can scold yourself for him."

"That's what brothers are for."

"But he's not really your brother."

"In every sense but biological, Ryan is my brother. I'm not going to let a little thing like a bloodline keep me from enjoying what I have."

Alexis smiled. "I like that, too."

"Hey, my family's a barrel of fun."

"I see that."

"And we're a barrel of fun pretty much because this is how Angus trained us to be."

"I can see that, too."

She said it objectively so that Cal would understand that she wasn't necessarily softening toward Angus, but that she would at least be fair. As far as she was concerned, that was probably the best first step toward getting him to admit he liked her.

Because he'd finished eating, Cal lay on the blanket and

plopped his Stetson over his eyes. "So tell me everything there is to know about advertising."

"Why? So you can fall asleep?"

He removed his hat far enough to peer at her. "I'm not going to sleep, I'm getting in my listening mood. I'm curious about the business that has you tied up in knots and yet completely captivated. I guess I want to know why."

Here was the second good step to getting him to admit he liked her—telling him about herself, her life. In fact, thinking about it, she realized she and Cal had gone about this relationship the wrong way. They skipped the getting-to-know-you stage and went straight for wanting to sleep with each other. It was no wonder they were confused.

She drew a long breath. "Well, I began working in advertising when I was in high school. My mother had started her small PR firm to get out of the house a few hours a day. She had enough business to keep her busy, but she also didn't want to miss time with me, so she arranged for me to come to her office in the afternoons and work for her."

"Somehow or another, I thought she had a staff," Cal said from beneath his hat.

Alexis shook her head. "No. In the beginning it was just her and me."

"Hmm," Cal said noncommittally.

"In college, I started taking advertising and marketing courses right off the bat. Basically that was when we started expanding. At one point, I think my mother hired an account executive only to give me a teacher. He went out and drummed up the business and then I helped him fulfill the campaigns. Eventually it got to the point where Jess and I were working together as a team more than as a mentor and student, and we hired Montana."

Cal lifted his hat long enough to peek at her. "Montana?"

"His mother loved Westerns. Anyway, Jess got the business, Montana came up with the ideas and I managed everything, and I do mean *everything*. From coffee for clients to finding new space when we got too big. When I graduated from college, I realized I was running the show, not my mother, but no one really said anything. Montana got a better job and was replaced by Phyllis. Jess started his own agency and was replaced by Chuck. Phyllis went to work for Jess, and Chuck found Ivan.''

"Sounds more like a soap opera than a company."

"That's the way it is sometimes."

"It's no wonder your business went under. You can't keep training new people and keep a business going."

"You can in advertising. You have to. People switch jobs all the time. It's part of the game. It's part of the way a company gets fresh ideas and part of the way people get ahead. The really good people are always being enticed away, and I had a knack for finding the really good people, giving them their basic training so to speak and then sending them off to bigger, better things."

"You never switched jobs."

"I own the company...or at least half. My mother gave me half interest and made me president when I graduated from college. If I feel the need to learn something new, I simply bring in new blood."

"Odd business."

Alexis grinned. "You bet."

Cal lifted his hat again. "And you love it."

This time Alexis laughed gloriously. "Absolutely."

"And I'll bet right now you could go back to the house and come up with something really profound."

Though she hadn't thought it possible to get her tired, dragging brain working again today, Alexis discovered Cal was right. She did feel energized and ready, as if she could conquer the world.

"Do you want to run back or do you think you can tolerate the slowness of the Jeep?"

Alexis laughed again. "You did this deliberately, didn't you?"

"What? Fed you?"

"No, got me talking about what I love and why I love it so that my brain would click again."

He tapped her nose with his index finger. "Honey, I'm not that smart."

The hell he wasn't, Alexis thought, admiring him as he walked to the Jeep with the picnic basket. And not only was he smart, but he was also sensitive. And he'd listened. He didn't just get her talking for the sake of getting her to open up so she'd loosen up and be able to create again. No, he'd gotten her talking, then listened to and commented on every word.

Her heart gave a funny little catch. He'd said there was no hope for them, but he was wrong. She *knew* he was wrong.

All they needed was a little time.

Chapter Eleven

"So what do you Texans do when it rains?"

"Probably the same thing as you New Yorkers," Cal answered, glancing up from the daily paper he'd bought in town that morning. "We bake cinnamon rolls."

"Oh, you do not!"

Cal shrugged casually, then went back to his paper. "Hey, a man can try."

For a good minute and a half Alexis wished she could make cinnamon rolls. Thanks to Cal's impromptu picnic, Alexis had written until four in the morning. Using the wonders of her computer she'd created the concept for the entire *Diet Splash* campaign. She'd drafted ads, written potential scripts for commercials and even chosen possible actors and models to bring it to life. All she had to do now was package it and get it to an overnight delivery carrier. The only problem was, she didn't have a clue where the overnight delivery drop-off was.

Boy, she really wished she could bake cinnamon rolls.

Cal must have heard her deep sigh, because his paper rattled, then he peeked over the top at her. "Problem?"

"Yes... No. I'm okay." She hadn't forgotten what he'd said about his last girlfriend taking over his life. Though the two situations were entirely different, Alexis realized Cal was still looking for reasons to keep her at bay. She wasn't about to hand him any ammunition.

"Why aren't you in the den working?"

"I'm done."

"You don't have other clients you could attend to?"

"Not really."

He shook his head. "Crazy company."

"Crazy business," she admitted readily. "We already went over all this yesterday."

"So we did."

Because the conversation faded away, Alexis could hear the sound of the clock ticking. She glanced around, knowing that as far away from everything as they were, if she didn't get her package on its way soon, it wouldn't be in New York tomorrow.

Cal's paper rustled again.

Alexis paced to the window. She supposed she could take a car and go into town. Surely somebody would know how to ship a package by overnight...

"You want me to entertain you, don't you?"

"No," she said, but it came out more as a gasp. Unfortunately his question reinforced her decision not to ask too much of him too soon. If he thought she was depending on him, he might feel trapped again. "No. Read your paper. I'm fine."

"Then stop sighing."

"Oh, I'm sorry. Am I sighing?"

"Only about every thirty seconds."

"Sorry, it's just that...that I need to get this package out today," she admitted reluctantly. "I don't want to bother you, but I haven't a clue how to find the local overnight carrier."

Cal rose from his chair. "Frankly I don't have a clue,

either, but I'd say Madison probably does. Federal Express and UPS trucks live at her corporate headquarters. So, let's just go to her office and get your package moving."

"I'm sorry."

That stopped him. He turned and faced her again. "For what?"

"For bothering you. I'm always bothering you. First, my car broke down, and I ruined your vacation since you couldn't leave because I was here…"

"Honey, I could have left the second day after you arrived. I knew you were exactly who you said you were. I knew you weren't going to steal the silver." He paused, caught her gaze with his. "I stayed because I wanted to."

A shiver of excitement rippled through Alexis. Without any prodding, he had admitted he wanted to spend time with her. Soon, very soon, he would see there was something more than lust between them.

All she had to do was stay cool and wait. He would come around. And when he did, she would be ready.

"It's no problem," Madison said cheerfully as she took the carefully wrapped package from Alexis's hands. She pressed a button on her telephone and brought her secretary into the room. "Lilah, would you please take this to the mailroom and see that it's shipped overnight? Instructions, address and phone information are all on that top sheet."

Young, energetic Lilah smiled enthusiastically and left with Alexis's package. Alexis felt as if a huge weight had been lifted off her shoulders.

"I'd love to give you a tour of my facility," Madison offered.

But Cal shook his head. "I'm sure Alexis has other things…"

"No, actually, I don't. I have nothing but time while I wait to hear about this campaign," Alexis said and rose from her seat to indicate she was ready to go. "I'd love a tour."

"Cal?" Madison asked curiously.

Cal rose, too. "I have nothing better to do."

He said it casually, calmly, but he watched her. Alexis noted with growing awareness that his gaze rarely strayed from her. At first, that made her edgy, nervous. Now she knew he was studying her because she fascinated him and he was past the point of denying it.

A sweet burst of satisfaction coursed through her. Everything was moving along right on schedule. Any day now Cal would admit he liked her and once he said the words she would... She would what?

She would do what? Alexis demanded of herself, walking beside Madison as she began to show off her second pride and joy, her business. Smiling and nodding politely, Alexis pretended she was interested—and composed—though she was far, far from it.

If Cal asked her to, she realized, she'd give up anything— maybe everything—for him. She'd give it up quickly and perhaps with less than adequate consideration.

She'd been so intent on getting him to admit he liked her that she'd forgotten she hadn't spoken to her grandfather in eighteen years. There was no telling what kind of sparks would fly when she did. She had also forgotten that her mother had no one else but her. If she decided to live with Cal, what would her mother do? She had also forgotten that she had a company to save, employees who depended on her.

And she had also forgotten that if Cal seduced her, he didn't have to ask her to stay; her grandfather had committed her to Texas for the next year. Cal could seduce her, and even keep her, without having to make a commitment at all.

"Madison has quite an impressive facility," Cal observed

after Madison had spent two hours showing them her corporate offices and the adjoining plant.

"Yes, she does," Alexis agreed, striving to sound normal.

In the final analysis, Alexis realized that most of her concerns were simple problems, easily solved by a decision or two, except for the fact that her grandfather had set it up so Cal didn't have to commit himself to her.

She was impulsively, recklessly ready to give her heart to a man who hadn't asked for it, and probably wouldn't have to.

"Something wrong?" Cal asked quietly, as he walked her to the car.

Alexis swallowed. "No. Everything's fine."

He stopped walking and caught her gaze. "You know, you have an exasperating way of insisting everything's fine when I can see a storm brewing in those pretty green eyes."

Striving for control, for common sense, for a link with logic, Alexis said, "My whole life has been turned upside down in the past few months. There may be a storm in my eyes forever."

"I've seen your eyes very calm," Cal reminded her, then spontaneously brushed his lips across hers. Not passionately, but sweetly, as if to offer succor.

Alexis's limbs went weak. If anything, she found his sweetness much more intoxicating than his sensuality—though he had that in abundance.

He pulled away slowly, watching her eyes. "So, I'm guessing that the reason you're troubled now is that you're thinking about things you can't control."

The absurdity of the truth of it made her smile. "You couldn't be more right." If there was one person she knew she couldn't control it was him. If there was one person she didn't want to control it was him. If he came to her, if he loved her, she would want it to be his choice.

It couldn't be any other way.

"Since you need to take your mind off your worries, I say we keep the tour going."

"Keep the tour going?" she asked curiously.

"Well, you've seen the town's major employer, Madison's corporate office and plant. Next I can take you to the sheriff's office. After that, we'll hit the diner for supper, and you can go back to New York telling everybody you've seen the entire town of Crossroads Creek."

"I'm sure they'll be impressed," she said calmly enough, but her stomach clenched. If she had any doubts about Cal's intentions, the subtle way in which he summoned her back to New York was enough to clear them up. He might like her, he might want her, she might even intrigue him, but he saw her going home.

"Great. Jailhouse, first," Cal said, slammed her car door and rounded the car's hood.

When he opened the driver's side door and jumped inside, Alexis said, "Jailhouse?"

"Caboose. Hoosegow," he said, laughing as he started the engine of the Cadillac. "Haven't you ever seen a Western?"

Thinking about her former employee Montana, Alexis grimaced. "No. And from the sounds of things I'm glad."

"Oh, they weren't so bad. A little...well, a lot off the mark, but they served their purpose. They were entertaining."

"And the cowboy myth lives on," Alexis agreed, realizing she was living, breathing proof of how women were nearly helplessly attracted to the rugged masculinity of a man earning his daily bread doing manual labor. Of course, she wasn't merely attracted to Cal because he was gorgeous, or because he had muscles culled from hard labor. She was attracted to him because he was sweet, sincere, generous, genuine and wonderful.

He proved that to her again when they arrived at the sheriff's office and Annabelle Parker nearly fell into a fainting swoon at his feet. Though the woman was almost comical in her devotion to him, Cal was neither impressed with it, nor dismissive, showing Alexis that he had enough respect for Annabelle that he took her seriously.

"I heard the good news about Grace," Annabelle said, wide-eyed with excitement. "It's all over town that both Madison and Grace are pregnant. Ryan's so happy I caught him putting smiley faces on parking tickets."

"I thought it was a nice touch," Ryan casually explained as he pretended great interest in something on his desk.

"Smiley faces are for sissies and geeks!" Cal groaned, lightly shoving Ryan.

"Face it, Cal," Ryan said, then began to laugh. "We are entering the world of sissies and geeks. We're no longer cool. We are the next generation. It's our turn to rule the world."

Though she was happily taking her mind off her troubles, listening to the interplay between two men raised like brothers and a woman who'd gone to school with them, lived in the same town with them and knew their deepest, darkest secrets, Alexis came to attention. "What did you say?" she asked Ryan.

"I said it's our turn to rule the world," he answered with a laugh.

Flabbergasted, her mind working as furiously as a computer hacker trying to get in before getting caught, Alexis looked from neat as a pin Sheriff Ryan Kelly—tall, handsome, committed, dedicated and about to be a father—to Cal who was also tall, handsome and committed and dedicated to those *he* called family... Both in their thirties, raising or about to raise the next generation of kids. The people guarding our towns, producing our food, building the buildings, marrying our women, having our children...

"Oh, boy, I wonder if it's too late to get that stuff back from Madison's shipping department?" Alexis said then fell to the chair beside Annabelle's desk.

''Why? What's wrong?'' Cal asked, immediately at her side as if he sensed something terrible had happened.

''I just had a vision of the real *Diet Splash* campaign.''

''You've already written the real *Diet Splash* campaign,'' Cal cautiously reminded.

''No, I wrote what I thought they wanted to see. Then, just now,'' she said, looking again from Ryan to Cal. ''I saw the real campaign. The one I told you had been in my head all along but I couldn't get it to come out.''

''Here we go,'' Cal said to Ryan who only started to laugh.

''Hey, I have been here, I have done this,'' Ryan said and reached for Cal's Stetson from the peg behind his desk. He tossed Cal's hat to him. ''Get her to a computer, give her coffee, don't expect her to get any sleep tonight.''

''Anything I can do?'' Annabelle asked soberly.

''I'm not sick,'' Alexis said, but she didn't protest as Cal led her to the door. ''I just have a really great idea and I need to get home to work.''

''I'll drive fast.''

Alexis didn't come out of Angus's den for two days. In that time, Cal provided pot after pot of coffee. Each day he made her breakfast, lunch and dinner. The second day he nearly fed her all three, because she'd let all three sit the day before. She didn't deliberately ignore him. In fact, every time he came into the room they talked. They discussed how far she'd progressed. She told him about pouring her heart out onto paper and how, from the ramblings she scribbled, she would choose themes and directions. She told him about refinements. She told him about turning themes and refinements into actual scripts and print ads. But she never showed him the ads. She couldn't. She'd actually used him and Ryan as the actors. And if he saw that, if he saw how much she respected and admired him, he'd also see that she loved him.

"So what you're telling me is that you're done?"

She smiled, nodded. "Very, very done. Completely done. And completely brilliant."

"Why don't you tell me how you really feel about this campaign?" Cal teased with a grin.

"Cal, all I can tell you is that this was inspired. This was one of those lucky breaks an artist sometimes gets. I worked and worked and worked in what I considered was the right direction and then suddenly, without warning, after I thought I was done, I realized the idea had been right under my nose all the time. And it's brilliant."

"So, you said," Cal observed, crossing his arms on his chest. "Are you going to sit? I mean, ever? Or are you going to pace for the rest of your life?"

Alexis couldn't help it, she laughed. "I'm so full of nervous energy I may never sit again."

"Three pots of coffee will do that to you."

"I know. I feel so weird. I'm so tired my muscles ache, yet I can't sit."

"You need a hot bath."

"I don't even think that will help."

"Let's try it anyway."

As he led her from the den and up the stairs, Alexis began to feel the tiredness that creativity had kept at bay. By the time they reached the top of the steps, she felt as if she could drop where she stood and seriously wondered if she'd make it to her room.

"Just a couple more feet," Cal soothed as he directed her down the hall, but Alexis felt her legs giving out from under her. The minute the sensation swept over her, Cal scooped her up in his arms.

Dimly she experienced the sensation of being held against his rock solid chest. She smelled the wonderful combination of man and outdoors. She felt the strength of him as he held her, the steadiness as he walked.

"Cal?"

"Hmm?" he asked, opening her bedroom door and striding inside.

"I have to thank you."

"For what?" he asked, and set her on the yellow-and-white patchwork quilt on the bed. Awash with sunlight that filtered in through white lace curtains, the cherry wood bed and dressers gleamed.

"Well, really, you and Ryan gave me this new idea the other day."

He grinned. "No kidding? So, Ryan and I are sexy enough to appeal to your soda drinkers."

Fighting the sleepiness, she shook her head. "No, you and Ryan are nice enough to appeal to my soda drinkers."

He frowned and began taking off her shoes. "Nice? I didn't want to be nice. I wanted to be sexy."

"Oh, you're that, too," Alexis assured emphatically. "That's the whole deal. The combination of sexiness and innate goodness. If that doesn't sell soda, I don't know what will. You're strong, you're smart, you're intelligent, you're good and you're still wickedly, wickedly sexy."

"Alexis, you're very tired," Cal said slowly. "And as much as I like hearing you say all these things…"

"What? You don't think you're wickedly, wickedly sexy?"

Still kneeling, he grinned again. "Well, maybe one wickedly, but not wickedly, wickedly."

She touched his cheek. "Oh, no. You're definitely wickedly, wickedly sexy. Sinfully sexy. Wonderfully sexy," she said and traced her finger along the line of his day-old stubble. She hadn't realized that in taking care of her, he'd neglected himself, which only made him sexier, sweeter. Lord, the combination was enough to drive any sane woman crazy.

She looked into his eyes and saw him staring at her. In that second, every ounce of tiredness she felt disappeared and in its place came bone-melting awareness. She wanted to make love with him, right here, right now. She wanted to feel him stretched out along the length of her. She wanted to touch all those hard muscles, all that solid flesh. And she wanted it to last forever.

As if reading her thoughts in her expression, Cal glanced down at her mouth. He'd taken off her shoes and knelt in front of her, his elbows braced on the bed, on either side of her hips. Only about a foot of space separated them, and the ideologies that seemed to separate them only a week ago had long since been modified or dispelled. As she wrote her *Diet Splash* campaign, depicting him as honest and good, she realized he wouldn't cheat her by taking advantage of the fact that she lived with him to keep his feelings for her from developing. He would be honest with her and do the honest thing. If he cared about her he wouldn't play games—and if he didn't care about her he wouldn't play games. Either way, she was safe with him.

Keeping her gaze fastened securely with his, Alexis held her breath, waiting. If what she believed was happening between them really was occurring, then he'd kiss her right now.

Cal didn't disappoint her. He seemed to debate for another few seconds, maybe weigh what he felt transpiring between them, then slowly, his gaze clinging to hers as if waiting for a protest, he bridged the gap between them. He touched his full mouth to hers softly at first, tentatively as if testing the truth of what they felt for each other. Then, with his mouth still on hers, he pushed himself off his knees and Alexis backward on the bed.

Even as she heard the creak of the mattress and felt herself sinking into it, she felt herself sinking into the kiss. The velvet softness of Cal's mouth on hers, the strength of the body that pressed her into the bed, and her own clamoring needs ebbed and flowed around her, taking her common sense and her reason and turning both into nothing but feeling and sensation. In a movement of liquid lethargy, she slid her hands up his arms, touching the firmness, the solidness of him, then across his broad shoulders. Helpless, her fingers tunneled into the thick hair at his nape.

All the while he kissed her.

His lips toyed with hers, drugged her. Her world dwindled down to yearnings and needs. Physical pleasures expressing emotional ties. She didn't try to stop her hands when they greedily began to explore him. She didn't even consider stopping his hands and they stroked and soothed, bringing her pleasure, taking her to planes of need she hadn't realized existed. She kissed him, touched him, and with every fiber of her being loved him...

Loved him.

God, she never knew she could love somebody so fast or so hard, and certainly not so completely in a few short days.

"Alexis, if we don't stop now, we aren't going to stop."

She pulled in a long breath. "I know."

"And I know that you've worked for two days straight. You're exhausted. You're euphoric. And you also somehow think I'm responsible."

Sighing, he angled himself away from her, then twisted and fell to his back beside her on the bed. "We both know this is wrong."

Having him say that hurt, but she gathered her courage and her wits and whispered, "I'm not exactly sure that it is."

"Then maybe this is the wrong time and the wrong place," Cal suggested evenly. Without giving her a chance to argue that, he pushed himself off the bed. "You get some sleep. If you still feel the same way after eight hours of sleep and a hot meal, then we'll talk."

He strode out of the room, and Alexis lay in the silence that followed. Her body still hummed with sexual pleasure. Her mind was reeling. Her emotions had been shattered. On the one hand she understood what he had been telling her. Maybe this was the wrong place and the wrong time and maybe they needed to think about this and maybe they needed to get to know each other better.

And maybe he didn't feel for her what she felt for him, Alexis realized miserably. If this was merely a question of time and place, if he could think that logically, that coherently, then he didn't feel what she felt.

Overwhelming, all-consuming, passionate love.

He didn't love her. It was that simple.

It gave her no comfort to realize she'd been right. When push came to shove, he had done the honest, honorable thing. He didn't take advantage of her.

When Alexis awakened it was to the sound of slamming car doors. Confused, she perked up. Listened again.

Voices. Muffled, but distinctly male and female.

Laughter.

Genuine laughter.

A pain squeezed around Alexis's heart. It was Cal laughing. He was happy to see the woman who had arrived.

And he didn't love her.

And she'd nearly made a fool of herself by not only giving him her body, but she'd also been ready to make praising declarations of undying love.

She shut her eyes. Lord, that would have been embarrassing, she thought, ignoring the pain of it for the more logical, more manageable emotion.

She quickly, unequivocally made two decisions. One, she wanted a shower. She didn't immediately need to go down to face Cal and the woman who made him so happy. But she did eventually need to face them. She needed to see, and to be reminded, that she was a new person in Cal's life that he already had a life, and that though she might be a part of it, she wasn't everything to him. Which meant he couldn't be everything to her. She had to regain her perspective. She had to get herself back to the real world.

Still, that didn't mean she would go downstairs looking

like a poor, downtrodden, cast-off. No. She decided she was going to go downstairs looking absolutely wonderful. He might have every right not to want her, but that didn't mean she didn't have the right to make him regret what he was throwing away.

She put on her peach halter, white slacks and strappy sandals. She fluffed her hair, added only enough makeup to look interesting and not so much anyone would notice she'd put any on, then—taking a long, deep breath for courage—made her way downstairs.

"Cal?" she called brightly, suddenly realizing that—if nothing else—the appearance of his visitor saved them from an uncomfortable scene. She knew they'd discuss this. She knew they had to, but at least it would be later after both were somewhat comfortable with each other and after the episode itself had time to diminish somewhat in significance.

"Cal?" she called again. "Did I hear we have company?"

"Yeah, Alexis," Cal said, meeting her at the bottom of the foyer stairway.

She pasted on her happiest smile and looked him right in the eye, as if to tell him the incident of him rejecting her meant nothing because she had been tired. But instead of seeing the indifference she expected, his eyes smoldered with unanswered need. Her breath caught, but when feminine footsteps sounded in the corridor to the den, the expression in his eyes quickly changed.

"Well, you certainly don't look any worse for the wear," he observed casually.

"When I heard we had company, I decided I should shower and dress so I don't embarrass you in front of your friend."

"My friend?" he asked, sounding confused.

She felt her face redden. "I could hear you and a woman laughing, Cal. It's not a crime. It's a good thing. I understood what you were telling me upstairs. You have a life. I might have intruded, but you still have a life."

"And that's what you think?"

"Wasn't that what you were telling me?"

"Yes," Cal began reluctantly, but before he could finish, Alexis's mother appeared behind him.

"Alexis! Darling!" she said, passed Cal and reached out to give Alexis a hug. "Cal told me about the new campaign. I'm sorry, but when I didn't hear from you, I thought you were brooding about Terry or your grandfather or something and I caught the first plane, next charter, shuttle and then rental car I could to get here."

Though she knew her mother intended for her to laugh at her description of the difficulty of getting to the ranch, Alexis felt her face go ashen. She felt her heart slow and then speed up to an unbelievable pace. Her eyes met Cal's for a second, but he looked away.

Chapter Twelve

"So, come on, darling, tell me all about it," Rachel said and began leading Alexis to the den.

Unable to stop herself, Alexis looked back and saw Cal staring after her. His eyes narrowed for a fraction of a second, then he plucked his Stetson from the rack by the door and headed outside.

"He *is* something," her mother cooed as they entered the den, arm-in-arm. "Sweet, decent, sexy as all hell..."

Alexis cleared hear throat. "I know. Actually he's my campaign."

"What?" Rachel asked as she took a seat on the burgundy sofa and patted the cushion beside her. "This I have to hear."

Trying to gather her wits, Alexis studied her mother. She knew she resembled her mother. Both had nearly black hair, both had green eyes. But until this minute, Alexis had never realized how young her mother was. Because Rachel was sixteen when Alexis was born, she was now only forty. She didn't have a gray hair or a visible wrinkle. Daily workouts kept her body trim and toned. Though Alexis had always suspected Garret Elliott wanted Rachel as his wife because she was an incredibly attractive woman—a nice fixture to have on his arm, a good trophy—Alexis had never seen the significance of that. Even now, Rachel MacFarland Elliott was quite a catch for a man who was in his fifties and balding, but even more of a catch for a man who had a bad temper and friends who were only friends because they were also business associates. Alexis couldn't recall one person who stayed in Garret's life beyond their professional association. She couldn't think of even one loyal friend. She couldn't remember anybody who stood by him.

Funny, how seeing her mother and thinking about Cal had caused Alexis to realize just how deficient her stepfather was.

"There's not much to tell," Alexis admitted hesitantly. "Cal's very handsome and very sexy, but his real appeal comes from the fact that he's stable, dependable, kind, generous and good-hearted. When I saw him and his brother standing together at the sheriff's office a few days ago, it hit me. Sexiness alone isn't good enough anymore. We're tired of being disappointed. Sexiness coupled with dependability, that's the good stuff. That's what we want to see."

"That's excellent," Rachel congratulated, clearly impressed, but also thrilled for her daughter. Until this moment, Alexis had also never really understood how supportive her mother was or how committed she seemed to be to help Alexis be the best she could be. Which explained to Alexis why she felt so compelled to save her mother. They were best friends. Because Garret subtly limited the things Rachel could do, the causes with which she could become involved, the hours she could spend away from him, Rachel lived a limited life, and the person to whom she was the closest was her daughter. That's how and why Alexis knew so much more, saw so much more, than a typical daughter might know or see. And that's why Alexis felt duty-bound to do something. She was only returning the favor her mother had given to her all along…support.

"The campaign is just excellent," Rachel continued to praise. "Are you going to get Cal to model?"

Alexis couldn't help it, she laughed. "I don't think so."

"He's perfect," Rachel said.

Alexis shook her head. "He'd rather be shot."

"So, you've asked?"

"I don't have to," Alexis said, then began to prowl the room. As perceptive, as intuitive, as she and her mother were about each other, Alexis also recognized that it wouldn't be long before her mother would sense something happening between her and Cal.

Alexis had made a mistake with Cal, a big one, and she wasn't even sure what it was. She might have misinterpreted what he'd said when he refused to make love to her—and she could understand that and even forgive herself because she had been exhausted—or maybe she'd insulted him by insinuating that he'd kiss her when he had another woman.

"I don't have to ask him," Alexis repeated, looking at her mother. She'd puzzle all this out later. For now, though, she didn't want her mother interfering. She didn't even want her mother suspecting. Until she got this straightened out with Cal, she had to make her mother believe her interest in Cal was purely professional. "I know him well enough to recognize that he'd think it foolish or stupid, or maybe just a waste of his time and he'd be right. His time is too valuable to spend it standing in front of a camera. Once we get the essence of his personality on paper, we can get any sexy actor to give us Cal's style."

"Hmm, yes," Rachel agreed. "You're probably right."

"I know I'm right," Alexis said firmly, then she brightened. Her plan had accidentally worked out beautifully. Not only was her mother away from Garret's influence, but she was at the ranch. The home that Rachel had pined for almost two decades. "But what about you? What did you think of the ranch?"

Rachel didn't even try to lie. "It's breathtaking. It's awe inspiring. I didn't realize how much I missed it until I saw it." She paused long enough to catch her daughter's gaze. "Alexis, when I pulled in, something tightened in my chest. I had so many memories I couldn't catch them all."

"Now, do you see why I wanted you to come down?"

Rachel laughed. "Yes. I definitely do, but I'm not so stupid that I don't see that this is overwhelming." Tired, she rubbed both hands down her face. "I'd need days—no, weeks—to absorb it all. And I don't think we have days before your grandfather returns. What are we going to do if he gets here before we leave?"

"I don't know," Alexis said and began to pace again. "But, Mom," she said haltingly, "I'm having second thoughts about everything," she admitted honestly. "Did you know Angus raised Cal, Cal's sister Grace and the town sheriff, Ryan Kelly?"

"You've mentioned bits and pieces of that."

"They are three of the most kind, most generous people I've ever met," she said and thought of Cal. Of how he was always there for her. Of how he took in Terry before Alexis even realized he should. "I can't think of Grandfather the way I have for the past eighteen years. It doesn't compute anymore. I feel like I should give him a second chance."

Rachel stiffened. "You do?"

"Oh, Mom," Alexis said and walked to the sofa where she knelt in front of her mother and took her hands. "Can't you see? We'll learn more about Grandfather by the people around him, than by anything he says or does."

"Deserting us wasn't an easily forgivable thing."

"I can't help but feel there has to be an explanation for that..."

"There is."

Both Alexis and her mother gasped and turned to see the

man who made the simple statement. A tall man in his late sixties who was losing his graying hair, Angus MacFarland nonetheless held himself proudly.

Rachel shakily rose. "Dad."

"Rachel," he said, standing in the doorway, not making a move to come in. Not saying anything more. Hardly breathing.

Alexis scrambled to the door. "Grandfather," she said and impulsively hugged him. She couldn't hate anyone who had made Cal the man he was. She took him in her arms, feeling his arms go around her, and knew, absolutely knew, as Cal had suggested and as Angus himself had said, there was an explanation.

"Alex," Angus whispered, cupping her cheeks in his big hands. "Alex." He hugged her again, tears streaming down his face, and Alexis couldn't help but cry, too. So many years had passed, so much grief, so much wasted time. And for what? What had kept him away?

She pulled back again and studied his weathered face. He would tell them, but on his terms and in his time. Right now he was waiting for a response from Rachel and unless he got the right one, everyone would go back to waiting again. Alexis licked her lips and stepped back. As if by magic, Cal appeared at the den door.

"Come on, Alexis, let's you and me go out and take a walk or something."

Alexis looked from her grandfather to her mother and then back to her grandfather again. She had as much right as anyone to this explanation, but she wasn't going to get to hear it.

Cal tugged on her arm. "Come on."

She looked at him. "I want to stay," she whispered as Angus started into the room.

"This part isn't any of our business."

"More of your country wisdom?" she asked sarcastically, because she was frustrated, not because she was angry.

"No. Good old common sense that even city people should have," Cal said and yanked her out of the room. Once she was clear of the door, he closed it.

"How do you expect them to settle a dispute when it's an unfair fight?"

"An unfair fight?" Alexis echoed stupidly, as Cal dragged her out the front door. "What the hell is that supposed to mean?"

"Well, in the first place, it would have been two against one."

"Hmm," she said, though she didn't agree, she did see his point.

"Then there's the fact that you were leverage. With you in the room it wasn't a father and daughter dealing with each other or solving a problem, it was a father and daughter and grandfather who'd hurt his granddaughter, and a mother with a disappointed, hurt child. The cards just kept stacking against him."

Alexis sighed. "I suppose." It hit her then that they had their own disagreement to straighten out, and now they not only had the time, they also had the privacy to do it. But she wasn't sure she could deal with it right now. Her nerves were jumping with worry. Her mind was reeling with possibilities.

"He said there's an explanation for everything that happened," Alexis said suddenly. Because of the swift pace Cal maintained, they'd traversed the space from the grass around the house to the land around the barn in a few short minutes. "What do you think that is?"

Cal shook his head. "I don't have a clue. All these years I thought your mother had run away and angrily refused to come home. One look at Angus's face this afternoon and I knew the problem wasn't your mother's but Angus's." He paused, hooked a boot on the bottom rung of the fence around the corral. "I've never seen Angus scared. I'm not sure what to make of it."

"He always treated you very, very well, didn't he?"

"He is unbelievably generous," Cal said truthfully. "What he did for me, my sister and Ryan amounts to no less than saving our lives. We didn't know it at the time. We didn't really appreciate it. Ryan rebelled every chance he got. But Angus stood by us. Made us into the people we are today. It boggles my mind."

Alexis sighed and looked up at the blue, blue sky. "It boggles mine, too, considering that I was living a life of absolute misery while he raised other people's kids. Whatever his reason," Alexis admitted, "I have a feeling it's a doozy."

At that Cal laughed. "Undoubtedly," he said, then looped his arm across her shoulders. "So, what do you want to do? We could ride, we could have a picnic, we could take a drive…"

"Or we could take my newest campaign to Madison's office and ship it overnight to the *Diet Splash* people," Alexis suggested with a grimace.

"Oh, you little workaholic," Cal said in a tone that was mockingly complaining. "What am I going to do with you?"

"I don't know," Alexis said suddenly, and stopped dead in her tracks. "What are you going to do with me?"

Cal could tell from the look on her face that her question was serious and that it also applied not to this minute but to everything, particularly the near miss on her bed this morning.

He drew a long breath to buy himself another ten seconds of time, then said, "You know that we're partners."

She nodded.

"You know that if you decide to stay here, we have to run a multimillion-dollar enterprise together, even as you try to run your ad agency."

She licked her lips. "Yes, I've figured all that out."

"If you decide to forfeit your share of the ranch now that

your mother is here and now that it looks like she and your grandfather might make up without your spending an entire year here, then you will go back to New York.''

She nodded again. ''Probably.''

''I won't live in New York.''

A statement of fact, not open for discussion. He watched her digest that, then reluctantly nod.

''So, you have to agree to live here for as long as we're together. And while you're living here, we'll be partners. So both of us would have to consider that. And, frankly, Alexis, I don't think I could be romantically involved with a business partner. It seems foolish and risky.''

''Yes, it does,'' she agreed hesitantly. ''So, what you're saying is that we can't have a relationship.''

''Actually, that's what it looks like,'' Cal said slowly. ''But are we sure we want to make that big, sweeping decision right now? Like this? Without a little more thought?''

If he loved her, he wouldn't have to ask that question. Since she'd fallen in love with him in less than two weeks and so completely that she had no question or doubt, Alexis knew that he didn't love her. Worse, if he didn't share this powerful, passionate, all-consuming feeling she had now, then she had to wonder if he ever would. And if he didn't, if he felt something that fell short of what she felt, would she want him? Could she be in that kind of relationship? Wouldn't it always feel one-sided? Could she handle that? Could a relationship survive that kind of strain?

No.

No.

If he didn't feel what she felt for him, then the strength of her feelings wouldn't be joy, they'd be something more like a prison.

''I don't think we need to debate it anymore, Cal,'' Alexis whispered. ''Frankly it's a no-win situation. If I stay and we're partners, we can't have a relationship. If I go, I'm in New York, and we can't have a relationship.'' With poise she was far from feeling, Alexis extended her hand for shaking. "So what do you say you and I just remain friends?"

He took one long, lingering look into her eyes, testing the sincerity of her words, she was sure. Keeping her slipping smile in place, Alexis confidently held his gaze, until he seemed to accept her decision.

"Deal," he said and finally smiled. When he smiled Alexis knew it was all over.

"Now, who the hell is that?" Angus bellowed when he saw a car barreling down the ranch lane, spewing dust everywhere.

Cal set his paper down. "I don't know," he said after glancing out the window at the dark colored Explorer. He knew the car was probably a rental, so he didn't put much stock in analyzing it. Particularly not when he didn't recognize the man who jumped out.

Angus gasped. "Sweet Lord, it's Garret Elliott."

"Rachel's husband?"

"Simpleton," Angus spat. "Here just in time to contradict my story before Rachel's had enough time to let it sink in."

Cal knew exactly what Angus was saying. "Hard not to believe the man you've been married to for eighteen years."

Angus snorted. "Particularly when the father begging forgiveness has a hell of a lot to be ashamed of."

"Angus, you married the wrong woman."

"And then paid her off and told her daughter that she was dead."

"You told Rachel her mother was dead to protect her."

"Aye," Angus agreed. "And at the time it had seemed logical. Now, it seems tacky, domineering and overbearing."

"All the things you accuse Garret Elliott of being."

Angus thought about that for a minute, then headed for the front door. "At least, I don't have blackmail on my résumé. Elliott,'' he said as he opened the door and stepped onto the porch. ''Fancy seeing you after all these years.''

''Where are my wife and daughter?''

''You don't have a daughter.''

''You know very well what I mean!'' Garret yelled.

Cal leaned against the doorjamb. Garret Elliott was an unattractive man in his fifties. His gray hair wasn't the appealing, distinguished gray. It was dull, listless and lifeless. His hazel eyes were deep-set and nondescript. His complexion was ruddy. The thirty extra pounds at his middle made him look lazy and weighted down.

If Cal guessed correctly, it was a feather in this man's cap to have caught the heart of such a beautiful woman as Rachel MacFarland. From the way Angus related the story, Rachel was very upset with herself for having an illegitimate child and she was settling for second-best with Garret. He'd tried to talk her out of dating him, but Rachel was thrilled with the attention from such a prominent businessman. The only problem was Angus had discovered Garret Elliott's shady business dealings, and also knew that he was basically being run out of Texas under threat of indictment.

In the way that people with money frequently do, Garret knew he wouldn't be prosecuted for the things he'd done. He wasn't worried about that. What worried him was losing Rachel. So, to counter Angus's charges, Garret had gone in search of dirt on Angus and he'd struck the mother lode. Discovering that Rachel's mother was alive, that she'd been in and out of jail for extortion and various and sundry other charges, Garret had immediately turned the tables on Angus and told him that if he interfered in Garret's relationship with Rachel, Garret would tell her the truth about her mother…maybe even bring Rachel's mother back into her life.

Angus couldn't let that happen. Angus knew Rachel's mother would bleed Rachel dry financially, but more than that, she would destroy her emotionally. So Angus gave up

Rachel, rather than see her get involved with her mother.
He policed Garret to make sure he kept his promise and also
that he was good to Rachel, and he waited eighteen years,
thinking he'd never see Rachel or Alexis again, but that
spring Rachel's mother had died and Angus had decided to
set everything right.

The only problem was, no one really knew what right
was anymore.

"Where's my wife?"

"Your wife, my daughter, is upstairs in her room with
Alexis. I told her everything."

"You idiot."

Cal stepped forward, fully intending to punch this guy if
he said another word to Angus, but Angus stopped him with
a wave of his hand.

"Is that any way to treat your father-in-law?"

"You're not my father-in-law."

"Oh, yes, I am. Blood is much thicker than water. You
can't erase those lines. Now, after today, I'm not sure
Rachel will want to. She may not want me back, but she
can no longer blindly hate me. And at least I have the satisfaction of getting her away from you."

"If she wants to go," Garret said with a sneer. "I might
not be a prince, but I've made Rachel happy."

"Alexis doesn't think so," Cal interjected from his position of leaning on a porch rail. He deliberately looked calm
and composed, so that if and when he needed to strike,
Garret Elliott wouldn't see it coming.

"And what the hell does that little snot know?"

"Well, for sure she hasn't yet figured out that you somehow screwed up her business."

"Cal," Angus gasped. "Don't be leveling any more ac-
cusations than we already have to deal with."

"Alexis recognized Rachel was unhappy. In fact, to hear
Alexis tell the story, I think she knew Rachel was unhappy
for a long, long time and growing even more so recently."

"That's a lie," Garret spat.

Cal shook his head. "I don't think so. I think she figured it all out as she was working with her mother. I also think you realized that because Rachel and Alexis's ad business was making money hand over fist it was only a short time before Rachel and Alexis both realized they didn't need you anymore. I think you saw that they were on the verge of leaving. So, before things went too far you did the thing you do best, you interfered. I don't know how you did it, I don't know what you did, but you did something."

"And you can't prove it," Garret cockily reminded Cal. "So, let's just deal with the things we can prove."

"No, I'd like to know how you ruined my business."

"Alli," Garret said, but rather than the nickname sounding sweet, Garret sounded as if he was whining. "Surely you don't believe what this guy is saying."

"He never really said anything," Alexis reminded, walking out of the house and onto the porch. In an unexpected show of support, Angus put his arm around her. Alexis took strength from that. "But you never really denied anything, either. You simply told Cal he couldn't prove anything. So, what is it he can't prove?"

"Sniveling little brat," Garret said, angrily. "You are as ungrateful as my parents always said."

"You mean, I'm as ungrateful as your parents always complained," Alexis said. "Nothing I ever did was good enough. Then, when I finally had something good, something successful, you took that away from me," she said incredulously. "All the things I thought I'd imagined I now realize were true. You didn't want me, your parents didn't want me. All you wanted was my mother on your arm."

"You look here, missy, I loved your mother."

"No, Garret, I don't think so," Rachel said, joining her family on her father's porch. "If you really loved me you would have accepted Alexis. And I think that's the thing that bothered me all along. All eighteen years. You made me think that it was you and me and Alex against the world, but when the chips were down you didn't want Alexis coming on vacations, or going to the theater, or doing anything with us. At first, I thought it was her age. Then, when she grew older, more lovely and more refined, I couldn't find an excuse for why you always excluded her.''

"We were a couple," Garret said in exasperation. "Couples don't always take their kids everywhere.''

"But you didn't want kids," Rachel said as if only now remembering. "You didn't want our children, you didn't want my child. You weren't anything you pretended to be, Garret, and if I'd been thinking clearly instead of always giving you the benefit of the doubt I would have seen it years ago.''

Garret sighed heavily. "Rachel, come home. Let's talk about this at home.''

Rachel only lifted her chin. "Garret, I am home. I'm sorry I didn't see it sooner.''

With that she turned and walked into the house.

"You'll hear from my lawyer," Garret yelled after her.

Rachel stopped, smiled. "I'm looking forward to it. Let's see, half of everything you own should make me a rich woman.''

"You witch..." he shouted after her, storming onto the porch.

Cal took one step to the right and blocked his way. "I don't think so.''

"I'll get you for this.''

Alexis shook her head. "No, you won't. You can't hurt us now. Because if you try, I'll look into the misconduct allegations from the year you were dating my mother. See if there's a statute of limitations, see if there's reason to prosecute.''

Standing side by side with Alexis, blocking the entryway to the house, Cal tried unsuccessfully to control a smirk. "I think she's got you," he told Garret, then pointed to his rental car. "I also think good manners should take you off the ranch right now before I have to call the sheriff."

Huffing, furious, Garret stormed away. He drove his car out the lane in the same cloud of dust that brought him in.

Cal turned to Alexis. "Well, kid, you did it. You brought your mother home, you found out why she was so unhappy, you made your grandfather very happy..."

Suddenly the truth of it all hit Cal, and he realized that this more than anything else might have been the reason he'd stopped them upstairs only hours before. Alexis was a strong, determined woman and, though he certainly didn't fault her for that, he knew that with as much as he felt for her already, if he allowed her the opportunity to get even further under his skin, he'd never get away from her. She'd have him so addicted, so captured, that he'd never be free.

He thanked his lucky stars he'd had the foresight to stop them before they took those final, drastic steps. Then thanked his lucky stars, he'd remembered the logical, concrete reason of their partnership that forced them to keep their heads about this relationship. Because for as much as he wanted her, he refused to need anyone, and Alexis was the kind of woman a man would easily, happily grow to need.

But Cal didn't want to need anybody.

He knew better.

Chapter Thirteen

That evening, right before dinner, when Grace told Angus she was pregnant, Alexis watched her grandfather's face crumple with emotion. She watched him fall into his old burgundy chair. She watched him bury his face in his hands and weep.

Alexis realized the reasons for Angus's weeping ran much deeper than becoming a grandfather for the second time. In one day, his daughter had returned and had reunited with him. Then his adopted daughter arrived and announced she was pregnant. It almost seemed that every wish he'd ever had was coming true all at once.

Alexis glanced at her mother and noticed Rachel studying Grace. Grace was a tall, poised woman, willow thin, with sable-colored hair and eyes the color of a storm-washed sky. Her husband, Nick, a black-haired, solemn-eyed man, was also tall. His dark, dark eyes never left his wife, but though the expression in them was serious—earnest—broader, brighter emotions hovered just beneath the surface. It was easy to see Nick Spinelli adored Grace; and easy to see the reverse was true as well.

And equally easy to see that Rachel approved of Grace. Alexis's mother wore a look of quiet endorsement, as if Rachel realized Angus might not have made it through the past eighteen years without Grace, Cal and Ryan, and she appreciated everything Angus's makeshift family had been for him.

"What time are Ryan and Madison arriving?" Angus asked, then noisily blew his nose.

"I asked them to be here at about seven," Cal replied from the doorway. "Which means I'm going to need some help with these steaks...Nick?"

"Yeah, sure, I'll help," Nick readily agreed. "Grace, you coming with me?"

She shook her head. "No, I think Angus and Rachel and I should spend a few minutes catching up."

"So, do I," Alexis decided and rose from her seat on the burgundy leather sofa. She wanted her mother to have an opportunity to settle in. She wanted her mother to feel the real part of this family that she was. "Besides, I'm better with the salad than Cal."

Though he was halfway down the hall, Cal turned and gaped at her. "Nobody makes a salad like I do."

"Precisely," Alexis agreed and was rewarded by a quick burst of laughter from everyone else in the room.

"You do have a tendency to throw in everything but the kitchen sink, Cal," Grace said through her laughter.

"That's what makes my salads unique."

"And sometimes barely edible," Nick said, slapping Cal on the back. "Come on, let's go tend to the steaks. We'll leave the salad to the women."

"*Woman*," Alexis corrected him, and noticed that Cal gave her an odd look. It was a combination of longing and regret that coupled with resignation, as if he had resigned himself to something he couldn't change—Alexis stopped her thoughts. She and Cal had made a clean break, which both of them realized was for the best. She wasn't letting one sad look hook her in again. Losing him the first time hurt enough. She'd be foolish to hang on.

After washing the salad vegetables, she considered staying in the kitchen if only for self-preservation, but recognized this was now her family, too. The Triple Moors was her home. No matter how difficult, she had to face Cal, to deal with him as a friend, and part of her grandfather's family. She took her washed vegetables, croutons and other ingredients out to the patio with the men who were grilling, and within minutes Grace joined them, arm in arm with Ryan.

"Where's Madison?" Cal asked, realizing—as everyone appeared to—that Grace had left the den to give Rachel and Angus more private time.

"She took Lacy in to see Angus. I suspect she'll be out in a minute…without her daughter."

"I'll bet Angus loves Lacy, doesn't he?" Alexis asked.

"Angus just loves kids," Ryan said.

"And he really didn't get to have any," Alexis added quietly. "Except my mother."

When the patio grew silent, it was easy for Alexis to see how much Angus's children loved him and how much they suffered for him. They were a wonderful family. Everything she'd dreamed of growing up. Everything she'd been deprived of because Garret Elliott was a snake.

"But Angus had his compensations," Nick said, filling the awkward silence. "And it seems like everything's working out."

Because Nick looked to her for confirmation, Alexis smiled. "Appears to be. I know my mother's got a lot to go through, a lot to deal with, as far as Garret and her crumbling marriage are concerned, but I also recognize that she believes her father."

"And what about you?" Grace asked casually, snapping lettuce into Alexis's bowl.

"What about me?" Alexis asked uncomfortably.

"What are your plans?" Ryan asked indifferently, as if he were only making easygoing conversation, but Alexis felt oddly as if she were being grilled for answers.

"I don't know," she replied honestly. "I guess I have a lot to think about, too."

"Well, you've got all the time in the world to think, and a very quiet, very relaxing atmosphere in which to think about it," Grace said.

"Unless the *Diet Splash* people call," Cal interjected from the grill.

"You came up with the campaign!" Grace happily said. "Congratulations!"

"Actually I came up with two," Alexis admitted with a grimace. "The second was better. I sent the first one, got the second idea, and had to call my client and tell him the second, better idea was on its way."

"I don't know," Madison said, coming through the door and onto the patio. "I thought the idea I saw was pretty good. What could you have possibly done to improve on it?"

"I completely rewrote it," Alexis said, laughing.

"New focus?"

"Entirely. I decided to hit everybody over the head with commitment, dedication, strength of character...and sexiness."

"Oh," both Grace and Madison said.

Nick and Ryan looked at Cal, who rolled his eyes and shrugged.

"And you think this one is better?" Nick asked doubtfully.

"I think this one reaches the target audience," Alexis said and got a resounding second from both Grace and Madison.

"You think commitment is sexy?" Nick asked, still skeptical.

Grace rose from her seat and kissed his mouth. "I know

I'm going to think you're adorable when you're waking up in the middle of the night to change our baby's diapers.''

"Now, don't you go saying you agree," Ryan ordered Madison. "For the two weeks we lived together in that cabin, you wouldn't even let me touch Lacy let alone feed her or change a diaper."

"Because I didn't want you to be sexy to me. I didn't want you to be domestic and sweet and nice. I wanted you to be mean and distant. I couldn't very well give you a chance to show me you were sweet, now could I? Otherwise I would have fallen in love with you even quicker than I did."

"All this is starting to confuse me," Ryan said and turned to Nick and Cal. "How long until the food is done?"

"Any minute now," Nick said, obviously relieved. "You're not buying all this stuff about housekeeping making a man look sexy, are you?" he asked Ryan in a whisper.

Ryan shrugged. "Damned if I know."

Cal barked out a laugh. "You guys are being set up and you don't even know it."

Both Ryan and Nick stared at him. "Well, hello, Mr. Pot calling the kettles black," Ryan snarled. "It's your woman who put this idea in everybody's head."

Cal colored uncontrollably. "She's not my woman."

Nick burst out laughing. Ryan coughed and looked away.

Cal almost denied it again, on principle, but decided saying nothing was better. At least that way he could hope the subject would be dropped before Alexis and the other women heard what they were talking about.

A few silent seconds went by before, confused, Nick finally said, "Why not?"

"Why not what?" Cal asked, feigning ignorance.

"Why isn't she your woman? Are you blind?"

"No, what I'm not is stupid."

When Nick only stared at him and Ryan frowned, Cal sighed. "Look, we're partners, remember? We own a mul-

timillion-dollar ranch. Unless or until we get that straightened out, we can't be anything.''

Nick said, ''Hmm.''

Ryan kind of nodded and looked away as if he didn't
believe Cal but he also didn't want to argue.

''Then there's the fact that she could be going back to
New York,'' Cal reminded both his brother and his brother-
in-law because he felt he needed to add weight to his argument.

''And you couldn't go with her?''

''Not if I wanted to run the ranch.''

''You couldn't even go for a week or so at a time?'' Ryan
asked craftily.

''I could. But I wouldn't want to. This ranch is my life,''
Cal reminded both Nick and Ryan. ''If any two people
should know that it's you two.''

Ryan grunted noncommittally. Nick bobbed his head.

''What is with you two?'' Cal asked angrily. *Had everybody but him forgotten about Becky Ann Quinn?* ''I make
a concrete, logical, sound decision, and my two best friends
obviously don't agree with it.''

''Oh, I agree with it,'' Nick said.

''So, do I,'' Ryan also said. ''It's just that the whole thing
is so dispassionate…I almost feel sorry for you.''

''Sorry for me?'' Cal gasped. ''Sorry? *For me?*''

''Yeah,'' Nick said, as if he'd only now figured out that's
what he was feeling. ''I've never been happier than I have
over the past few months. I can't imagine why you'd run
from this.''

''How about losing control of your life?'' Cal asked angrily. ''Do you mean to tell me that you don't mind that
you've lost control of your life?''

''I haven't…'' Nick began.

But Cal interrupted him. ''The hell you haven't! And the
hell you haven't,'' he added, pointing at Ryan. When he
realized his voice had raised enough to draw at least passing

attention from the women, he lowered it. "You might have been ready to give up your freedom, but I'm not."

"And you think Alexis will take your freedom?" Nick asked quietly.

"I know she will," Cal emphatically stated. "For the past two weeks I've done nothing but run after her, keep her company, make her happy. Not that I minded, once I settled into the routine I enjoyed most of it, but I just feel that it would get worse."

Standing only about a foot behind them, off to the left and hidden by a tall bush, Alexis felt all the blood rush to her feet. All the time she'd thought Cal was doing things for her because he liked her, all the times she thought him sweet and considerate, he was only humoring her. Doing things he felt he had to do.

Her rational mind realized his fear of losing his freedom and being imprisoned had more to do with his past bad relationship, but she was so overcome with emotion that she didn't *want* to be rational.

She didn't remember asking him to do anything for her.

She didn't remember bossing him, being demanding, or behaving badly.

She didn't remember stealing his freedom.

She didn't want his freedom.

She didn't want anything from him.

Anything.

Not ever.

Chapter Fourteen

Alexis waited until Ryan and Madison had gone, Nick and Grace had been comfortably settled into one of the guest rooms, and her mother and Angus had retired to their respective sleeping quarters before she slipped onto the back porch where she knew Cal was taking his nightly look at the stars. As she'd found him on her first night at the Triple Moors, Cal sat on the top step, his back braced on the weathered wooden pole that held up the porch roof.

"Can I talk to you for a moment?" she asked quietly.

"Yeah, sure, Alexis," he answered and invited her to sit beside him on the step by patting it. "Have a seat."

"No, I think I'll stand for this."

She knew it was the tone of her voice that caused him to give her a puzzled frown, but she didn't care. She fully intended to have her say, and then she'd consider them finished. "I never asked for your help. In fact, when I first arrived, I was doing everything for myself and a good many things for you, including caring for Terry. Don't ever tell anybody you don't want anything to do with me because you're afraid I'll steal your freedom. I never asked for your help. I don't want your freedom. You can have your freedom. In fact, you can stick it in your ear.''

With that she turned and started into the house but Cal must have leaped from his seat because he caught her before she made it into the kitchen.

''Eavesdroppers never learn anything good about themselves.''

''Yeah, well, if you were an honest man I wouldn't have had to have heard this from eavesdropping,'' Alexis informed him coolly. ''But, frankly, none of it matters. Somewhere along the way you got the impression that I was trying to steal your life, or change your life, or run your life, when nothing could be further from the truth. I never asked you to do anything for me. Most of the time I thought we were partners of a sort, doing things that needed done together. How dare you insult me in front of your family by insinuating I'd made you do things you didn't want to do.''

''I never said that!''

''You didn't have to. You clearly implied it. But now that everything's out in the open, neither one of us has to worry about the other getting a mistaken impression again. Not only do I want absolutely nothing to do with you, but if you dare lift a finger for me again, I'll go to my grandfather and insist that you not be allowed within twenty feet of me for the entirety of my visit.''

Cal squeezed his eyes shut and blew out a long stream of air, as if angry with himself and having difficulty controlling it. ''Alexis, you have this all wrong.''

''Fine. Wonderful,'' she said, crossing her arms on her chest. ''Then explain to me what you meant.''

Cal opened his eyes and for a few seconds only stared at her as if debating his answer. Finally he said, ''I don't think it's fair to have to explain. And that's part of why I don't want to get involved in a relationship. I like you a lot, much more than I thought I could like anyone, but I've been down this road. I know that permanent relationships are like prisons. I know they eventually turn people against one another…''

Her lips trembling, Alexis said, ''Then you must be very worried about Grace and Ryan. Or upset that they're in such terrible prisons.''

Cal raked his fingers through his hair. ''They're different.''

''Oh,'' Alexis said, nodding. ''I see. Since the variable in our relationship is me, then I must be some kind of horrible shrew who will cut off your freedom and make you answer for every move you make.'' She paused, considered, then added, ''I don't seem to remember ever doing any of that in the weeks I've been here, but, then again, what do I know? I'm only the other half of this equation, the half you didn't bother to consult before you made all your decisions about me and about any relationship we might have had. I'm not anybody at all.''

With that she turned and walked into the house and Cal let her go, then squeezed his eyes shut. Why was it that he couldn't explain to Alexis that he was keeping them a safe distance apart for her good as well as his own? Did she want him to confess that she wasn't the problem, he was? Did she want him to admit that *he* was weak-willed. That if he loved her, he'd never let her go, either? That she'd lose her freedom every bit as much as he would?

Cal awakened the next morning to the scent of pancakes and two things struck him immediately. First, this was probably the last day of his vacation and, second, somebody other than Alexis was cooking.

The very thought of Alexis caused Cal's stomach to tighten, but he ignored it. Of course, this hurt. They were a good team. They liked each other a lot. And, unfortunately, they were incredibly sexually attracted. It wouldn't be easy to give up or ignore all those temptations, but it was for the best.

He reminded himself of that sage wisdom when he entered the kitchen and saw Alexis, her hair pulled into a ponytail, her short shorts exposing her long, long legs and the blouse tied at her midriff accenting the soft curves of her body. Attraction hit him like a bolt of lightning, not just because she looked adorable and sexy as all hell, but also because she looked so damned right standing in front of the stove—making pancakes that weren't burned.

"When did you stop burning things?" Cal asked, confused.

Grace gasped. "Cal!"

"Oh, it's all right, Grace," Alexis nonchalantly said as she placed a stack of pancakes on the table. Grace and Nick sat side by side as did Rachel and Angus. Everyone had already eaten their first helping, and though Rachel and Grace had settled in with coffee, it was obvious Nick and Angus planned on eating another round. "Your brother thinks I'm an idiot. I burned a few things the first few days I was here. After that I got accustomed to the stove and never burned anything else, but he only remembers bad things."

"Son, it's never polite to insult anyone's cooking," Angus reminded, "unless you'd like to pick up the spatula and take over."

"Good point," Cal said, diffusing the argument because he couldn't believe a simple comment had turned into such a disaster. Alexis had never taken his insults to heart before, but he supposed since they were now among other adults he'd have to be more careful about what he said, in order not to offend her.

"Your pancakes are very good," he offered, instead, after he'd taken his first few bites and confirmed that opinion.

Alexis smiled. "Stick them in your ear," she said, then walked out of the kitchen.

Four pair of confused eyes turned their gazes on him. Cal looked from Rachel, to Angus, to Nick, to Grace, then sighed heavily. "We actually got along much better when no one was here."

"I certainly hope you didn't make a habit of insulting her, boy," Angus said.

"I didn't insult her. In fact, once Ryan reminded me that we needed to keep Alexis here until you got back from fishing, I took fairly decent care of her."

"You took care of her?" Rachel asked, puzzled. "Alexis doesn't let anyone take care of her. She's so independent that I'm surprised she let you lift a finger."

"Well, for a while there she didn't," Cal reluctantly agreed and began to understand why Alexis might have been angry that he'd given his brother and brother-in-law the impression that he'd taken care of her. He'd forgotten how independent she was. It was no wonder she was angry with him.

"So, what are your plans for the day?" he asked Angus, deftly changing the subject because he didn't think it was anybody's business but his and Alexis's. He knew he was going to have to apologize. He knew he was going to have to straighten this whole mess out. But he just didn't want to do it with an audience.

"What are *your* plans for the day?" Angus countered.

"Isn't it my last day of vacation?" Cal asked carefully.

"Not hardly. Since you didn't take the trip I gave you all bets are off. You and I have a lot of catching up to do." He paused, turned to Rachel. "What are you going to do today?"

Rachel sighed. "I don't know. I have so much to think about. Alexis was right. I had been hiding my misery for years. Now that I realize I don't have to be miserable anymore, I have some decisions to make."

Cal didn't hear too much beyond Rachel's admission that Alexis was right. She'd been right about a lot of things. But she'd never rubbed his nose in any of his mistakes. Aside from the episode this morning, she was actually easy to get along with.

He was definitely going to have to apologize to her. Actually, he was going to have to explain.

"Okay, Cal, let's go," Angus said and rose from his seat, rearranging Cal's plans for the day. "First we'll check out everything that was done while we were away. Then, we'll look around and see what wasn't."

Though Cal would have much rather hunted for Alexis to apologize, he knew he couldn't say no to Angus. Instead he headed for the foyer, grabbed his Stetson from the peg and met Angus on his way to the barn.

After a very cordial, very happy dinner, with all three of Angus's "adopted" children, Rachel and Alexis, all gathered around Angus's table, Cal surprised Alexis and quietly invited her outside.

Her heart tripped inside her chest and she nodded casually. While it appeared that no one was looking, he led her out to the patio.

The black sky was awash with stars, a nearby wetland was alive with night sounds. Her heart pounding in her chest, Alexis turned to Cal.

"What is it?"

He sheepishly looked at the ground. "I need to apologize."

Her heart skipped a beat. "Oh?"

"Yeah, after our fiasco this morning I got to thinking that maybe you were right. Maybe I had inadvertently suggested that I'd taken care of you."

Alexis waited. When he said nothing after a few seconds had ticked by, she prayed there was more, but he remained silent.

"Well, since we've already hashed this out," she said maturely, calmly, though her emotions had been shattered. She was sure he had realized he'd made a mistake. Since he hadn't and since she'd already embarrassed herself enough, Alexis drew herself up to her full stature and pasted a smile on her face. "I can accept your apology without any further discussion. Thank you," she added then turned and walked into the house again. She almost returned to the happy family sipping wine in the living room, but changed her mind. In the morning if anyone asked her where she had disappeared to the night before, she'd plead a headache, but for now she simply had to get away.

Because it seemed that the really, really rotten luck that had brought her to Texas had finally caught up with her again.

"He what?"

"Grace," Alexis said, then laughed slightly. "Please. You're behaving as if you don't know your brother at all when it's clear to me that he doesn't want a relationship with anybody, and he doesn't hide that."

"But…"

Alexis held up a cautionary hand. "Please, don't you see that I'm trying to save face here. At least I know he has nothing against *me*. He simply doesn't want to settle down."

Grace sighed. "I know that's what he says, but I don't think that's true. He had a really bad relationship with a woman—Becky Ann Quinn—a few years back and since then he's been very careful. Becky had Cal wrapped around her little finger. I always thought that when the right woman came along he'd see that Becky was the problem, not him, not relationships in general."

Alexis laughed. "How do you know I'm the right woman? Maybe the right woman will come along and he will be fine," she said easily enough though the very thought splintered her heart with pain. "For now, though, let's let me save face."

"Alexis," Rachel called, as she walked down the hall. "Alexis."

"In the den, Mom," Alexis said, rising from her seat on the sofa and going to the door. "Back here."

"There's a package for you," Rachel said as she met Alexis in the doorway of the den. "It's from the *Diet Splash* people."

"Oh, great!" Alexis said, grateful to have something to do, something to occupy her mind, and maybe even a reason to return home. She didn't want the ranch anymore. She didn't need it. And the last thing she wanted to do was be partners with a man whom she adored but who considered her an annoyance.

With Grace over one shoulder and Rachel over the other, Alexis ripped open the package. Inside were her preliminary drawings, scripts and ads, red-penciled with the client's suggested changes and revisions.

As Alexis rummaged through the different information, noting that the changes and suggestions were few and far between, Rachel took the cover letter and began to read it. "Oh, my God, Alexis," she said, then fell to the sofa. "Look at this budget."

Alexis took the letter from Rachel's hands, read it and fell to the sofa beside her mother. "Oh, Lord."

Grace grabbed the letter. She read it, looked at Alexis and said simply, "This is a lot of money."

At dinner that night, Angus proposed a toast. "I know this is Grace and Nick's last night before they return home, but since Alexis got such good news today, I thought we'd celebrate that."

"What good news?" Cal asked without thinking.

"She got the *Diet Splash* campaign," Rachel answered proudly.

"Hey, that's great," Cal said, then remembered how she worked for it. How she struggled for it. How she deserved it. "So, when do we start?"

"If I decide to take it, I need to go back to New York to

make preliminary arrangements to shoot the commercials, while my staff works the bugs out of my ads and my scripts. So, you're pretty much out of the picture on this."

"Yeah, that's right," Cal said, looking down at his plate. He really wanted her to have this win. He knew she needed this win. He just didn't realize she would have to leave so soon—or how much it would hurt to have her leave.

"Well, the other half of the good news, Cal," Angus continued, completely oblivious to the dynamic taking place between the two people he'd unwittingly partnered, "is that Alexis is giving up her half of the ranch."

This caused Cal to look up sharply. Again he ignored Angus and looked directly at Alexis. "You're giving up the ranch?"

"If I leave for New York, I break my one-year condition of living here to get my share."

"I'm sure we could amend that," Cal said, glancing at Angus who looked willing enough.

Alexis smiled softly. "I don't want the ranch, Cal. And I know you do. So, enjoy."

Cal swallowed the lump that formed in his throat. This time last month he would have blamed his inability to speak on gratitude. He did love this ranch. He loved it more than anything and he wanted it. It was stability and continuity. But half had actually been enough. He didn't need to own the whole thing. He didn't mind having her as a partner.

"But I don't have time to be your partner," Alexis said, answering him though Cal didn't even realize he'd spoken aloud.

He drew in a quiet breath for composure. What was happening to him? "Well, I just want you to realize the offer is open," he said, covering his slip. "I don't want you backing out because you want me to have the ranch. Half is more than enough, as long as I have my home."

"Hear, hear," Angus agreed toasting. "To home."

Everyone around the table toasted with Angus and when

Alexis sipped she glanced at Cal over the rim of her glass. Though she was smiling, he saw the distress in her eyes and for a fleeting second he wished they were alone because if they were alone he could get her to tell him what was wrong. He stopped that thought. It was thinking like that that had gotten them into trouble in the first place.

But he spent the evening watching her. Outwardly happy, she said all the right things, made all the appropriate comments, answered each question the way Cal suspected it should be answered, but he continued to see that shadow in her eyes. By the time Ryan and Madison bundled up Lacy and returned home, Grace and Nick said good-night and reminded everyone they'd be leaving early in the morning, and Rachel and Angus slipped off to their rooms, Cal was ready to chew nails. He walked out to the back porch and waited, certain that Alexis would come outside to discuss her problem, but she never did. Luckily it only took him fifteen minutes to realize she wasn't coming.

Because he knew she wouldn't be asleep in so little time, he snuck upstairs, tapped twice on her door, then let himself in.

She greeted him with a gasp of surprise. "What are you doing here?"

Wearing simple sleeveless mint green satin pajamas, she was completely covered, yet somehow completely sexy to Cal. The pale color brought out not only the green of her eyes, but also made her hair seem darker, more luxurious. He decided to ignore how terrific she looked, how sexy and wonderful and downright perfect she looked, and focus on the real reason for his visit.

"I want to know what's wrong."

"What's wrong with what?"

"With you."

She sighed. "There's nothing wrong with me. I got a contract big enough to reopen my agency today. I'm going home tomorrow. You've got your ranch back. My mother has her life back. Angus has his family back. In case you haven't noticed, Cal, all is right with the world.''

He watched her through the entire dissertation and though she hadn't changed her facial expression or her tone, Cal still didn't believe her. ''Then why are you sad?''

''Who says I'm sad?'' she asked belligerently.

''Your eyes say you're sad,'' Cal said and began to advance on her. Jolts of awareness danced along his nerve endings, but Cal believed he could handle them. After all, things between him and Alexis were settled. All that remained was friendship, whether she wanted it or not, and he couldn't stand to see her so unhappy. At this minute, making her happy again had to take precedence over everything else.

''My eyes are probably saying I'm exhausted,'' Alexis argued tiredly, as she warily backed away from him. ''And I have a million things to do in the morning.''

It hit him then that she'd already told him she was leaving in the morning but he hadn't caught the full significance of that. ''Are you unhappy because you don't want to leave the ranch?''

She coughed out a laugh. ''Cal, this has nothing to do with the ranch and everything to do with the fact that I'm on my way home to a mess. I have a company to resurrect. Half my staff got new jobs. So I have people to replace and work to get done and new clients to find.''

''So you should be happy,'' Cal softly observed, then reached out and impulsively skimmed her hair with his fingertips.

''Damn it, I am happy!'' Alexis yelled, then drew in a long breath to calm herself. ''Get out, Cal.''

''No,'' he said, and watched her face change when his hand shifted from her hair to her cheek. She seemed to move into his palm even before he brought it to her face. ''I want to help you.''

"Oh, no," she said, but she said it weakly. "I'm not accepting your help, remember?"

"Then at least tell me what's wrong. Let me be a shoulder to cry on."

She would have loved to. She would have loved to have moved into his arms as he was trying to entice her to do. She would have loved to have admitted that she wasn't entirely sure she wanted to be a business owner anymore, that she'd rather be a creative consultant. She would have loved to have shared the pain and the joy of having her work, her creativity, her sweat and blood pay off. She would have just loved to have been able to talk to him.

But they'd tried that once and they both took different meanings from simple things, so it was better not to have any complications between them. Because he was a part of Angus's life and now her mother was a part of Angus's life, maybe even a permanent resident of the ranch, Cal would also be a permanent part of Alexis's life. It was best to get this settled now.

She slipped away from him. "Didn't you hear me, Cal? Everything's fine."

He caught her going around the side of the bed and trapped her between the cedar chest and himself. "I'm hearing that everything's fine. I'm seeing differently."

"Then get your eyes checked," she said breathlessly, wishing, aching to be able to sag against him. It wasn't that she didn't want to fulfill the commitments she had, it was more that everything was so much easier when she had someone to share it with. She realized in a flash of insight that she'd commute for him. She'd move her business to Texas and use faxes and modems and every other device known to mankind if it meant that she could have him in her life forever.

And that was dangerous. She was ready, willing and able to give up everything for him and he didn't even want her.

"My eyes are fine," he said softly.

"Then go have your head examined," she said, knowing that harshness was the only tool at her disposal now. If she weakened, even an iota, she'd be lost.

"My head is fine, too."

"No, it isn't," she insisted, hanging on to her control by the thinnest of threads. "If your head was fine, you'd be out of this room right now because…" she said, then swallowed hard to keep the real emotion out of her voice. "Because you're back to giving me the wrong idea again."

Obviously considering what she'd said, Cal stepped away from her. "Oh," he quietly agreed. "You're right."

He left her then and Alexis fell to the bed. Tears sprang to her eyes instantly and she let them fall. She'd done all this before. She'd been alone before. And she couldn't believe she feared going back to New York, running the company she loved.

No, she thought, shaking her head. She wasn't afraid. And it wasn't the work that bothered her. Losing Cal bothered her. In two short weeks she'd fallen in love with him, grown to depend on him, begun to appreciate his wit, wisdom and insights.

Maybe he was right.

Maybe, without actually noticing, she had been taking his freedom.

Chapter Fifteen

Because Grace and Nick were also leaving in the morning, it was decided that they would drive Alexis to the airport. In the background, leaning against one of the poles holding up the roof of the front porch, Cal watched unemotionally as Nick loaded the bags belonging to him and Grace. But he got an unexpected pang of something when Nick reached for the first piece of Alexis's white leather luggage. He couldn't help but remember the argument they'd had while unloading that very same luggage. Involuntarily he smiled. He thought he'd never learn to trust her, let alone get along with her. Now, here he was sorry she was leaving.

"Well, that's it," Nick said, slamming the door of his black sport utility vehicle. "It's time for us to get rolling."

"Okay, Nick," Grace called in return. "We're just about ready." She turned to Rachel and hugged her fiercely. "It was wonderful to meet you. Wonderful to have you here. I'll fax you directions to our home and I *expect* you to visit soon."

Rachel smiled. "I'd like that."

Grace moved to Angus. As she had done with Rachel, Grace also hugged him fiercely. "You could visit with Rachel, you know."

"I know. But maybe next time. I'd like my girls to get to know each other first."

Angus, Rachel and Grace began to make plans for visits, and though Nick and Ryan more or less stood in the background, nodding in agreement, Cal watched Alexis. There was a huge smile on her face, as if she were inordinately pleased with the job she'd done bringing her mother home and settling the problems with Garret Elliott, but Cal could still see the sadness in her eyes. It amazed him that no one else saw it. It amazed him that everyone believed she was happy—of course, he understood that everybody assumed she was happy about her *Diet Splash* campaign and chomping at the bit to get back to New York, but Cal suspected that she could handle the organization of that from the ranch. Yet, she still chose to leave.

"You watch yourself," Rachel cautioned Alexis before she hugged her goodbye. "I know you've lived alone in New York for the past two years, but don't get overconfident. Continue to be careful."

"I will, Mom," Alexis said, as if exasperated. Everyone around them laughed, but Cal narrowed his eyes. Why was it that no one noticed Alexis wasn't happy about leaving? Was he the only one who could see she was putting up a good front, but dying of sadness?

"Cal, come say goodbye," Grace beckoned and Cal uncrossed his arms and jogged down the steps. He grabbed his pregnant sister in a hug and swung her around once for good measure. "Have a safe trip," he said, then clasped Nick's hand to shake it.

"Don't worry," Nick said. "I'll be driving."

"Thank God," Angus said, obviously thinking of the fact

that Grace had demolished her car on her first drive up to Nick's home.

"You just won't let me forget that, will you?" Grace teased, as she slid her arm around her husband's waist.

Cal didn't know why, but he glanced at Alexis to catch her reaction to the happy interplay between Nick and Grace. He saw her look at them with longing and he suddenly realized why he could see that she was upset, but no one else could.

He was feeling the same thing she was. Longing. Sadness. She didn't want to go. He didn't want her to go. Because deep down inside, they loved each other. But there was a wide gulf of difference between them. They co-owned a ranch...or at least they did until she relinquished her half last night. The ranch was entirely his. Though, now that he thought about it, he supposed running the ranch with Alexis wouldn't have been that bad. True, they probably would have argued about some decisions but that would have been a good thing. He didn't always consider arguing to be arguing. Sometimes it was more like spirited debate. That's what he and Alexis had...spirited debates.

That is, when they didn't compromise. Looking back, he realized that he and Alexis had rarely argued because one of them always compromised. And if they couldn't compromise, they accepted each other. He'd accepted her buying plaid shorts for Terry. She'd accepted that Cal was a little old-fashioned. Cal had accepted that sometimes she needed comfort.

Not that comforting her had been bad. Actually he'd enjoyed it. Comforting her made him feel strong. Having her accept his advice made him feel wise, powerful, wonderful.

Without even trying, she'd given him a lot of gifts, Cal realized, watching his brother-in-law and sister say their final goodbyes and knowing that Alexis was undoubtedly saying her goodbye to her mother so she could be on her way with them.

Cal swallowed hard. God, he was going to miss her. He caught the shimmer of unshed tears in her eyes and he swallowed again. She was going to miss him, too.

But he couldn't help what he was. He didn't want to be trapped. He needed to be free....

Of course, she hadn't made him feel trapped. She made him feel good. He'd already admitted that. That's why losing her hurt so much.

Losing her.

He couldn't believe he was *losing her*. And not because she was pulling away, but because he was letting her go.

"Don't go."

He said it quickly, unexpectedly, and so loud the bustle of people huddled around the black sport utility vehicle quieted.

Gathering himself up to his full six foot four inches, Cal drew a long breath. "Don't go," he said again, this time directly to Alexis.

She stiffened. "I have to go."

"Okay, then, give me five minutes," Cal said, bargaining with her, enjoying it, finally understanding that that was what a relationship was all about. "Give me five minutes in the den. Then you can go."

He expected her to look to Nick and Grace for confirmation that they could afford the extra time, but she didn't. She stepped around her mother and grandfather and walked up the stairs of the porch. Her head held high. Without waiting for him, she entered the foyer and started for the den.

Cal scrambled after her. He could hear the murmurings of his family behind him, but he didn't care.

"What do you want?" she asked as he entered the room. Her heart had swelled so much when he asked her not to go that she wasn't even sure how it was beating. Fear and breathless anticipation had her in their grip. On the one hand she was terrified that she'd again misunderstood him. On the other, she still held the tiniest thread of hope that he wanted her. But she wasn't going to be so foolish as to misinterpret him. She would be on the next plane to New York, if he wasn't a hundred percent clear about what he wanted.

"I want you to marry me."

All her breath swished out of her lungs. "What?"

"I want you to marry me," he said simply, quietly.

She swallowed. "Do you know what you're saying?"

"Yeah," he said, then grinned. "Yeah. I know exactly what I'm saying."

"Then explain it to me because I'm not going to be caught short again."

"You and I make a really, really good team. We baby-sat Terry together. We handled the ranch while Angus was away. We got your mother down here. We took care of Garret Elliott. We even got your *Diet Splash* campaign where it was supposed to be when it was supposed to be there. I don't think you need to give up your half of the ranch. I think we can handle working together."

Alexis stared at him. "You want me to marry you to keep my share of the ranch?" she asked incredulously.

"No, because we work well together."

"Let me get this straight. You want me to marry you because we work well together?"

"Yeah, because I think that being best friends and being part of a team are the best two reasons to get married."

Alexis gaped at him. "You don't think sexual attraction and/or love are important."

"Oh, I love you," he said, then took the two steps that separated them, and pulled her against him. "And as for sexual attraction I think we have a little more than our share."

With that he kissed her, melting away all her worries and breaking down walls and barriers Alexis didn't even realize she'd erected.

When he pulled away, he framed her face with his big hands. "Alexis, I don't want to see you hurt anymore. I can't protect you from everything, no one can. But I'd be happy to do my best to try for the next fifty or sixty years."

Alexis wrapped her hands around his wrists. "And I can't protect you," she whispered back to him. "I know you were hurt. I know you're cautious because of it."

"Oh, honey," Cal said and began to laugh. "I didn't love her one-eighth as much as I love you, and today I finally figured out why."

Almost afraid to hear the answer, Alexis asked, "Why?"

"Because she's not you," Cal said, as if that answered everything. He pulled her to him for another quick kiss. "In a way she did me a big, big favor by making me so cynical for all these years."

Still reeling, Alexis said, "A favor?"

"Yeah, I probably would have married Wanda's sister if I hadn't been so difficult to get along with…"

Alexis stopped him with a scorching look.

"Kidding. Kidding," he said, then kissed her soundly. "You're the woman I love. You're the woman I want. And I'm ready for anything."

"Anything?" Alexis asked slowly, overwhelmed with love. Everything she'd ever wanted was finally hers. Her mother was safe, her business was booming and Cal was hers.

Hers.

"Anything."

"Okay, then," Alexis said with a laugh, linking her arm with his and directing him to the door. "As soon as we tell our families the good news, I'll have to call New York and begin the arrangements for me to work down here. I'll probably need another fax, a bigger computer and a drafting table. I should hire a secretary..."

Cal didn't really hear the rest of what she said, he didn't have to. Their lives would be noise, chaos and pure, unadulterated confusion for the next sixty or so years.

And he would love every minute of it.

Because in spite of everything her soft heart compelled her to do for everybody else, she loved *him*. She was his.

Epilogue

If there was one thing Angus MacFarland could say about his family it was that they weren't people to let grass grow under their feet. Madison and Ryan had produced a strong, healthy boy, Jordan, only a little over a year after they were married. Shortly thereafter, Grace and Nick had presented Angus with Olivia, a bright-eyed little girl. And, now, a few days shy of the first anniversary of her marriage to Cal, Alexis had gone into labor. She was early by three weeks, and everyone had been at a charity ball for one of Madison's causes, but no one had really cared. Once Alexis had given the word that things were progressing a little more quickly than she suspected they should, his family had packed up and headed for the hospital—tuxedos, ball gowns and all.

Leaning back on the worn plastic chair in the waiting room of the hospital, Angus marveled at how quickly his family could martial the troops. With Stella, Nick's former housekeeper, now Olivia's full-time nanny, baby-sitting Olivia, Lacy and Jordan, one phone call took care of the children. Because her labor pains were increasing at a rapid pace, Cal and Ryan had used the police cruiser and easily gotten Alexis to the hospital. Now, here they sat, Nick and Grace, Madison and Ryan, and Angus and Rachel, waiting for Cal to burst through the waiting room door with good news.

Looking around, a fission of pride skittered through Angus. With her sable hair pulled into a loose chignon, Grace, his adopted daughter, looked elegant and regal in the violet strapless gown. In a black tuxedo that made his black hair and brown eyes seem even darker, Nick was her perfect match. Beside them, blond-haired, blue-eyed Madison was the epitome of femininity in her pink beaded gown, but the smile on her face was for her husband, Ryan, who was dashing and sophisticated in his tuxedo.

All in all, Angus and his children had done very, very well for themselves.

And, yes, damn it, Angus shamelessly took most of the credit. If it wasn't for his pushing and prodding and sometimes downright scheming, he wasn't sure his children would have ever seen what was right in front of their noses.

Sitting beside him on one of the uncomfortable hospital chairs, was Angus's daughter and Alexis's mother, Rachel. Because they'd been waiting silently for the past twenty minutes, she squeezed his hand.

The waiting room door swung open, and Cal entered. He'd removed his tuxedo jacket, but still wore his white shirt and black trousers under his blue hospital coat.

"It's a girl," he announced, grinning like a fool. Gasping for joy, Madison and Grace ran over and hugged Cal. A little calmer, but still thrilled, Nick and Ryan slapped Cal on the back.

Without warning, Angus began to cry. *I'll be damned,* he thought, then let himself tumble into the emotion that swamped him. *This one really is a MacFarland.* He didn't realize how much that meant to him.

Weeping herself, Rachel put her arm around Angus's shoulders and he looked at her. His beautiful daughter was home again. His life was sane, sensible. Her life was sane, sensible. And they were getting grandchildren.

Everything was going to be okay.

*   *   *   *   *

If you enjoyed what you just read,
then we've got an offer you can't resist!

Take 2 bestselling
love stories FREE!
Plus get a FREE surprise gift!

Clip this page and mail it to Silhouette Reader Service™

IN U.S.A.	IN CANADA
3010 Walden Ave.	P.O. Box 609
P.O. Box 1867	Fort Erie, Ontario
Buffalo, N.Y. 14240-1867	L2A 5X3

YES! Please send me 2 free Silhouette Romance® novels and my free surprise gift. Then send me 6 brand-new novels every month, which I will receive months before they're available in stores. In the U.S.A., bill me at the bargain price of $2.90 plus 25¢ delivery per book and applicable sales tax, if any*. In Canada, bill me at the bargain price of $3.25 plus 25¢ delivery per book and applicable taxes**. That's the complete price and a savings of over 10% off the cover prices—what a great deal! I understand that accepting the 2 free books and gift places me under no obligation ever to buy any books. I can always return a shipment and cancel at any time. Even if I never buy another book from Silhouette, the 2 free books and gift are mine to keep forever. So why not take us up on our invitation. You'll be glad you did!

215 SEN CNE7
315 SEN CNE9

Name	(PLEASE PRINT)	
Address	Apt.#	
City	State/Prov.	Zip/Postal Code

* Terms and prices subject to change without notice. Sales tax applicable in N.Y.
** Canadian residents will be charged applicable provincial taxes and GST.
All orders subject to approval. Offer limited to one per household.
® are registered trademarks of Harlequin Enterprises Limited.

SROM99   ©1998 Harlequin Enterprises Limited

Silhouette ROMANCE™

SOMETIMES THE SMALLEST PACKAGES CAN LEAD TO THE BIGGEST SURPRISES!

Join *Silhouette Romance* as more couples experience the joy only babies can bring!

Bundles of Joy

July 1999
BABIES, RATTLES AND CRIBS... OH MY!
by Leanna Wilson (SR #1378)

His baby girl had suddenly appeared on his doorstep, and Luke Crandall needed daddy lessons—fast! So lovely Sydney Reede agreed to help the befuddled bachelor. But when baby cuddles turned into grown-up kisses, Sydney wondered if what Luke really wanted was *her!*

August 1999
THE BILLIONAIRE AND THE BASSINET
by Suzanne McMinn (SR #1384)

When billionaire Garrett Blakemore set out to find the truth about a possible heir to his family's fortune, he didn't expect to meet a pretty single mom and her adorable baby! But the more time he spent with Lanie Blakemore and her bundle of joy, the more he found himself wanting the role of dad....

And look for more **Bundles of Joy** titles in late 1999:

THE BABY BOND by Lilian Darcy (SR #1390)
in September 1999

BABY, YOU'RE MINE by Lindsay Longford (SR #1396)
in October 1999

Available at your favorite retail outlet.

Silhouette®

Available July 1999 from Silhouette Books...

World's Most
Eligible Bachelors

AGENT OF
THE BLACK WATCH
by BJ JAMES

Black Watch

The World's Most Eligible Bachelor:
Secret-agent lover Kieran O'Hara was on a desperate mission.
His objective: Anything but marriage!

Kieran's mission pitted him against a crafty killer...and
the prime suspect's beautiful sister. For the first time in his
career, Kieran's instincts as a man overwhelmed his lawman's
control...and he claimed Beau Anna Cahill as his lover. But
would this innocent remain in his bed once she learned his
secret agenda?

**Each month, Silhouette Books brings you an
irresistible bachelor in these all-new, original
stories. Find out how the sexiest, most-sought-after men
are finally caught....**

Available at your favorite retail outlet.

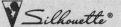
Silhouette®

THE MACGREGORS OF OLD...

#1 *New York Times* bestselling author

NORA ROBERTS

has won readers' hearts with her enormously popular MacGregor family saga. Now read about the MacGregors' proud and passionate Scottish forebears in this romantic, tempestuous tale set against the bloody background of the historic battle of Culloden.

Coming in July 1999

REBELLION

One look at the ravishing red-haired beauty and Brigham Langston was captivated. But though Serena MacGregor had the face of an angel, she was a wildcat who spurned his advances with a rapier-sharp tongue. To hot-tempered Serena, Brigham was just another Englishman to be despised. But in the arms of the dashing and dangerous English lord, the proud Scottish beauty felt her hatred melting with the heat of their passion.

Available at your favorite retail outlet.